tHe s

Biyi Bandele was born in Kafanchan, Nigeria, in 1967. He is the author of two previous novels, *The Man Who Came in from the Back of Beyond* and *The Sympathetic Undertaker and Other Dreams*. He has written plays for the Royal Court Theatre, the Royal Shakespeare Company, and for radio and television. He lives in London.

BIYI BANDELE

the street

PICADOR

First published 1999 by Picador

This edition published 2000 by Picador
an imprint of Macmillan Publishers Ltd
25 Eccleston Place, London SW1W 9NF
Basingstoke and Oxford
Associated companies throughout the world
www.macmillan.co.uk

ISBN 0 330 37539 3

1 3 5 7 9 8 6 4 2

A CIP catalogue record for this book is available from
the British Library.

Typeset by SetSystems Ltd, Saffron Walden, Essex
Printed and bound in Great Britain by
Mackays of Chatham plc, Chatham, Kent

In memory of Hakeem

The author thanks
The Wingate Foundation,
The Peggy Ramsay Foundation
And The Royal Literary Fund
Whose support was prompt
And most needed
In the period during which
This book was written.

And Iain Hutchison.
And Simi Bedford.
And Sarah Maguire.
And Edwin Salako.
Thank you all.

We fly to beauty as an asylum from the terrors of finite nature.

Ralph Waldo Emerson

BOOK ONE

THE STREET

1

On the morning of the day Nehushta finally phoned
Dada, several months after Dada had temporarily disappeared into his own mind and re-emerged feeling
like a landmine, or an oath of vengeance whose time
may come, two things happened: Dada had a strange
dream and his neighbour Haifa Kampana failed to
achieve an orgasm. Just after midday, the traffic lights
at the intersection between the High Street and Stockwell Road developed conjunctivitis. Taken each by
itself none of these three events would have merited a
footnote in the chronicle that continued to unfold that
day. But taken together they were, for Dada, like
clouds foretelling a storm in the wake of a severe
drought.

2

Dada dreamt that he was having dinner at Bah
Humbug, where he'd spotted Nehushta for the first
time not so long ago. When he awoke from the
dream, he could not remember if he'd been with a
friend, or by himself. All he could remember was the

waiter standing by his table as his eyes ran through the menu.

'No starters for me,' Dada told the waiter. 'I'll just have the main course.'

'I'm sorry, sir, but we've run out of starters.'

'Afters. Any afters?'

'Ah, desserts,' enthused the waiter. 'As you can see, we do have a rich selection of desserts, sir.'

'In that case, I'll have the starter, no main course, and no desserts.'

The waiter wrote down the order. 'Would you like a drink while you wait, sir? We do have an excellent selection of wine, cocktail and rum.'

'A coffee will do.' He was on the wagon.

'With or without?'

'Without.'

'Without what?'

'Without milk.'

'I'm afraid, sir, but we've run out of milk.'

'In that case, I'll have it without cream,' he said.

'Excellent choice, sir,' said the waiter, hurrying to the kitchen with the order.

A few seconds later, he came running back looking upset. 'I'm afraid, sir, but the chef has just informed me that we have in fact run out of wine.'

'In that case,' Dada said, 'I'll have a bottle of the house red.'

'Right away, sir,' the waiter said, scuttling off visibly relieved.

Dada over-indulged on the wine. He woke up from the dream with a piercing hangover.

3

In the flat next door, as Dada was coming out of his dream, his neighbour Haifa Kampana had a rude awakening: his body made an appointment that his mind could not keep. He gave up trying to seek relief for his customary early morning erection when, for the tenth time in half-an-hour, a hank of onions force-fully insinuated itself into his imagination and would not go away. Haifa had nothing against onions, but not so his erect member. The not so obscure object of its desire was not a bulb of several layers with a pungent smell, but an eighteen-year-old girl with a silver ring in her lower lip and a soft Scottish accent who worked at the tills of the Mezzanine (whose motto 'shoplifters will be beaten to death' was gener-ally taken at face value). Her name was Siobhan but Haifa didn't know this. And she was thirty, but that wasn't what she told him. She hadn't told him any-thing. He hadn't asked her anything. He'd simply assumed she was eighteen.

Haifa first set eyes on Siobhan one sulky winter evening when a thick fog hung over Brixton. He'd gone to her till and paid for the wrong kind of coffee. He realized straightaway that it was the wrong kind of coffee.

'Is that recaffeinated or decaffeinated?' he asked.

'Decaffeinated,' she replied.

'I'm sorry,' he said, 'I am allergic to decaffeinated coffee.' He paused, seeing her for the first time. 'You're new here. Where's Anna?' Anna was another girl who used to work the evening shift at this till. 'What have you done to Anna?'

Siobhan, whose nametag read Anna, pressed a buzzer and the store detective came over to find out what was going on. 'It's you again,' he said when he saw Haifa.

Throwing Haifa out of the store was a monthly ritual that he'd come to enjoy. The last time it happened was when Haifa bought a pint of milk and insisted on paying twice the price on the grounds that prices were so exorbitant at the store they might as well declare a permanent post-sales season: one-for-the-price-of-two. It might just catch on. 'What's the problem this time?' asked the store detective. Siobhan explained the situation to him. He turned to Haifa and carefully explained that there was no such thing as recaffeinated coffee. Haifa replied that this was a matter of opinion. The store detective had had this conversation with Haifa before. So he repeated what he'd said the last time. 'Opinions are cheap.'

'That's because they haven't been run through the tills of this store.'

'Look,' said the store detective as he ushered Haifa out, 'if you think our prices are a bit on the high side, why do you keep coming back?'

'Because this is the only store around for miles that's open twenty-four hours a day.'

'There's another one just down the road,' the store detective pointed out, 'at the petrol station.'

'I'd sack you for saying that to a customer,' said Haifa, 'if I was your boss. What's the new girl's name?'

'Anna.'

'The last girl was also called Anna.'

'It's the only nametag we've got.'

Haifa stared into the blue-grey eyes of the new not-Anna. And as she leaned forward to serve another customer, something disorientating and alchemical happened: her breasts, moving with the jerkiness and indescribable beauty of a time-lapse photograph, peeked out of her blouse, and stared back at him. It was a redefining moment in Haifa's life. He felt his manhood arise, slowly, tentatively, like a waif rising after a long stretch in the cold.

Haifa Kampana knew he was in love. He burst into tears.

4

Dada's hangover disappeared when he unleashed two shots of Hennessey on it.

A disembodied voice from the street, spiked with righteous anger, drifted into his flat.

'And when I go to court I said to de judge – my Lord, I 'ave already did smoke de cannabis but it's in me body and I don't have none! I'm say yes, me admit to guilt to say me did smoke it, I must tell you de truth. But I only smoke me little ganja, and do me little carpentry work.'

By the time he'd taken a shower and got dressed, it was well past midday.

The phone rang, as he was about to step out the door. It was Midé from the bookshop.

'Everything sweet?'

'Hanging in, Midé. Wuzzup? How's the world treating you this morning?'

'Like a baby treats a diaper,' said Midé. 'Listen to this one,' he continued. 'Two bulls run into each other one morning. One says to the other, "Yo, bro, heard the great news?" "What news?" asks the other. "The butcher!" exclaims the one, dancing around with joy. "The bastard's dead!" "Yeah?" says the other, unimpressed. "Has his butcher's knife died too?"'

Aside from selling books, Midé moonlighted as a stand-up comedian. He paused for a long time waiting for Dada to respond.

Finally he said, 'So, what do you think?'

'Is that a new one?' Dada asked, knowing he'd heard it before.

Midé answered him the way he tended to answer questions when he was pissed off: he didn't say a word.

'It's good,' Dada said.

'Good? Just good?'

'Midé, man, I really like it, honest.'

'You liked it so much you didn't even laugh.'

'You know me, Midé, I'm a "laugh quietly" sort of person.'

'No, I didn't know that about you, Dada.'

'Well, now you know it, Midé. Have you got hold of the book I ordered?'

Silence.

'Midé.'

'I'm still here.'

'I said have you—'

'I heard you.'

'And?'

'I answered.'

'I must have missed your answer.'

'Can't blame you, it was a silent reply.'

'Midé,' he said, 'tell me that joke again.'

Midé did. And Dada laughed till he was gasping for breath.

'The book is here,' said Midé. 'I'll hold it for three days.'

5

Brixton High Street was, as always, busy and frenetic, packed with the ever-present floating cast of the walking wounded and the clinically Undead; stricken men whose conscience hovered above them like flies over a banquet of dung; damaged souls haunted by memories of past transgressions and paralysed with guilt for sins not yet committed.

6

Dada made his way to the front of a crowd gathered by the tube station entrance around a big, heavily bearded man on a makeshift podium.

Mounted on an easel beside the man, who was a dead ringer for a man we know as Fidel Castro, was a board. And in neat, well-behaved handwriting the board declared:

My face is set, my gait is fast, my goal is Heaven, my road is narrow, my way rough, my companions few, my Guide reliable, my mission clear. I cannot be bought, compromised, detoured, lured away, turned back, deluded, or delayed. I will not flinch in the face of sacrifice, hesitate in the presence of the adversary, negotiate at the table of the enemy, pander at the pool of popularity, or meander in the maze of mediocrity. I won't give up, shut up, let up, until I have stayed up, stored up, prayed up, paid up, preached up for the cause of Jesus Christ!

Standing directly in front of the Bible-wielding Fidel Castro was a tiny, almost dwarfish man. This man – Dada's cousin 'Biodun – was known, to his friends and to his enemies, of which there were some, as the Heckler. He was known as the Heckler because, since he first showed up at the spot two years ago, it was all he'd been known to do: heckle. He was the ultimate nemesis of every man with a mission from God, every visionary with a cure for cancer who had set up a soap-box on the streets of Brixton. When he wasn't busy keeping himself in shape (which he did through a rigorous regimen of heavy drinking and chain-smoking) he was to be found wherever there was a soapbox, matching wits and trading insults with the wise men and women on a mission of mercy who flocked to Brixton every summer. He seemed to exist solely for these men and women who came every year to free the people of Brixton from a menu of ills ranging from 'the diabolical conspiracy of the western-capitalist hegemony', to 'the devil, the local council, the law, and intergalactic submarines'. Or to put to them crucial questions such as: 'Where does the light go when you cut the switch off?' leading on to the carefully articulated, 'Nubian Civilization *vs.* Western Syphilization: choose one.'

The Heckler locked horns with these mavens, gurus, roshis, lamas, shamans, revolutionaries, avatars, seers, illuminati, diviners, prognosticators, prophets and those who considered themselves the street clerisy. And, more often than not, he trumped them with his drink-fuelled erudition, his unequalled gift for devastating one-liners, his insightful analysis; and with utter and complete horse manure. It was said of the Heckler that if you locked him up in a room, he would find a way of picking a fight with himself. He was something of a celebrity in the neighbourhood, and had been told many times that his talent was criminally under-exploited in Brixton, and why didn't he relocate to Speakers' Corner on the other side of the river? He replied that the only relocation he would ever consider would be the relocation from Brixton to six-feet-under Brixton. He was born in Brixton, he said, and, although he didn't think he would live to see the day, he would die in Brixton. You see, he would say, his desire to see out his days on the streets of his birth had nothing to do with tribal loyalty and everything to do with thrift and his belief in the principle of Opportunity Cost. In other words, every time he saved a fiver by *not* travelling to Hyde Park he could spend that fiver on two pints of lager and a bag of crisps. Therefore the cost of *not* going to Hyde Park was two pints of lager and a bag of crisps. He didn't know about you, but he thought that it was a bloody good bargain *not* going to Hyde Park. In this way the Heckler started a trend amongst the impressionable youths of Brixton. They would go to a travel agent's and ask how much would it cost them *not* to go to Paris on the Eurostar Express this weekend? Answer: a pair of trainers.

7

'That's our problem!' the Preacher who looked like Fidel Castro was shouting. 'We can't do anything ourselves in order to deal with the problem. We are utterly unable to do anything. God,' – he gestured skywards – 'God did it for us!'

'Don't point!' shouted the Heckler. 'We know where your finger's been.'

The crowd roared.

The Preacher ignored him and continued, 'The Lord Jesus Christ left heaven—'

'He didn't leave heaven, he left a gay discotheque.'

' – came into this world, went to the cross . . . he was put on trial, and at this trial the judge said he was innocent. The Bible says he was tempted in every way like we are, yet he was without sin!'

'I'll have sin and tonic!'

'No one could accuse him rightly. Everyone who encountered him had to acknowledge—'

'What would have happened in Bethlehem if Mary had used contraceptives?'

' – Nicodemus, religious leader of the day, totally uninterested in spiritual things, had to say to Jesus Christ, "No one could do the things you do, unless he'd been sent from God."'

'What would have happened that night,' insisted the Heckler, 'if the Holy Ghost, when he descended upon Mary, had been wearing a condom?'

The Preacher paused briefly, thrown off his train of thought.

'There would have been no Jesus!' the Heckler shouted triumphantly.

'Jesus lived a sinless life,' the Preacher said, regaining composure, 'he went to death on a cross so that we could be made right. So that we could know forgiveness from sin.'

'I bet the Holy Ghost didn't find Mary's G-spot.'

The Preacher was beginning to get very irritated. 'I'm not talking about a laugh and a joke on Brixton High Street,' he said, careful not to look at the Heckler. 'I'm speaking about something tangible.'

'Yes,' responded the Heckler, 'would you move the platform closer to that tree. Pity, the rope doesn't quite reach.'

'I am speaking about something tangible that happens when the Lord Jesus Christ comes into your life, makes you new, cleanses you—'

'And buys you horrible pullovers for Christmas.'

' – The Lord Jesus Christ will come back from heaven and take those who love him, those who know him . . . he will take them home to be with him in heaven.'

'Off you go!'

'Ladies and gentlemen, you may laugh. You may joke—'

'Look, mate, if heaven's so wonderful, what the hell are you waiting for?'

' – but one day, each of us has to stand before a God who's just, a God who's impartial—'

'There's a bus leaving in five minutes!'

' – It won't be jokes! It won't be laughs. The only thing you can do is come to the foot of the cross. Not King's Cross, not Charing Cross—'

'Gerrard's Cross!'

' – the Cross of Calvary. The Lord Jesus Christ, nailed down on the cross, took my sin, took your sin and had it laid upon himself. You must come like Pilgrim in *Pilgrim's Progress*—'

'*Who?*'

' – to the foot of the cross, to have that burden rolled away. Here, in Brixton's own mini Speakers' Corner, everyone who comes here has something to say.'

'Yes, I have two words to say to you and the second one is "off!"'

'Whether they are a philosophy, whether they are a religion. Everyone is trying to point the way. Well, there is a very, very important question—'

'For you it's, is there life after death, isn't it?'

'When you're dead, you're done for. When you're six foot under, you're finished. But hang on a moment, folks, where do you go from here?'

'To the morgue, you moron!'

'Why do we die?'

'Because our heart and lungs stop working, you idiot!'

'Why are there tears? Why do people die?'

'To get away from you!'

'Our body gets old, we lose a few hairs, we go grey. The old eye crutches have to come out. The old hearing aid has to say, you know, can you speak up a bit. The body deteriorates.'

'Yours started a long time ago.'

'Man chose to sin against God. We can laugh about God when we've got life and health, when we've got breath in our lungs. But, folks, we're gonna die.'

'Good!'

8

In the aftermath of several riots, an urban-regeneration scheme known as the Brixton Challenge, which had been there all along but frozen in its tracks by gormless bureaucracy and conceptual incoherence, suddenly emerged from its lassitude. New businesses, restaurants, bars, a six-screen art-house cinema sprang up. Those who had lived through the nebulous years when Brixton was but a disease that officially did not exist and had given up trying to explain the place to visitors watched with interest.

In the New Brixton, the old mean streets had become the playgrounds and night-haunts of Trustafarians and Afro-Saxon literary, media and artistic types. As house prices in trendier neighbourhoods up north travelled to the Himalayas, many first-time homebuyers exfiltrated across the Thames and headed South.

9

'How's Auntie?' Dada asked the Heckler. They were at Helter-Skelter, one of the new café bars and restaurants that had sprung up within the past year.

Until two years ago the Heckler had a flat in Trinity Gardens just down the road. Now he lived with his mum, Dada's aunt, in the house where he was born on Ferndale Road.

The Heckler shrugged.

'I take it that means she's fine,' Dada said.

'There's the definition of an oxymoron.'

The Heckler ordered a jug of Pina Colada.

'The tab's on me,' Dada said wryly. 'Feel free to order anything.'

'Don't you get stingy on me, now. You know I'm broke.'

'I know you're broke. You're always broke.'

'Now tell me that's my fault.'

'It is your fault, coz.'

'Now tell me to go get a job.'

'Go get a job, brov.'

'There, you've said it. You've got the negativity off your chest. Feel better now?'

'What you don't seem to understand is—'

' – that life is hard.'

'Yes.'

'Compared to what?' The Heckler lit a cigarette. 'Everyting sweet?'

'How do you mean?'

'Still on the book hustle?'

'Yes.'

'Which is to say?'

'I'm finishing my book.'

He smiled knowingly and blew smoke in Dada's face. 'Neither am I. If you ever finish writing that book,' he continued, 'I promise to get a job. And not just any job. I'll become a priest. And that's my last lie for the day – here comes our order.'

He picked up the pineapple slice stuck on the lip of the cocktail jug and threw it into his mouth. He chewed loudly and swallowed it, flesh and peel. 'I love pineapples.'

'I'm starving,' Dada said. 'Wanna do lunch?'

'That was my lunch,' he said. 'I'm on a diet. I'm watching my height.'

'I thought we settled this last week. 'Biodun: you need to eat. You need your fucking food.' Dada's face settled into a grim, anxious smile as he looked across the table at his cousin.

'I'm not hungry,' said the Heckler looking away. 'I don't have an appetite.'

'Look at you, man. Thin as a rake and shorter than a bad temper. You know I love you, don't you, you crazy motherfucker.'

'Don't you be getting all emotional on me now, Field Marshall.'

'Cheers,' Dada said, pouring the drinks and raising his glass.

'Are we here to talk or are we here to drink?' the Heckler grunted as he washed down his lunch with the contents of his glass. He poured another glass, lit another cigarette and slumped in his chair, a catatonic look taking possession of his face as he stared vacantly on to the street outside.

10

On his way back to his flat after his look-see with the Heckler Dada came across the final segment in the trinity of signs that would later presage Nehushta's phone call that evening. He was standing with several other people by the traffic lights situated directly in front of the Police Station on the High Street. To his right was a veteran member of the Brixton Undead. He had a cigarette in one hand, a can of Special Brew in the other, and hanging from his neck a hand-written sign that said: 'Wife, three children and two dogs to keep. Please help.' To Dada's left was a well-dressed man staring at his own shadow as if it knew something he should know about. They were waiting for the pedestrian-icon to give them right of way. It took them several minutes to arrive at the conclusion that the light was simply mocking them, it had no intention of turning green. Dada turned to the man with the inscrutable shadow and, in the spirit of small talk on a radiant summer day, gestured at the red traffic light and said to the man:

'Is it broken?'

The man looked at Dada for a full sixty seconds before responding.

'No,' he said. 'It's got conjunctivitis.'

11

Dada crossed the street.

THE DREAM

1

One night, when she was thirteen, Nehushta's father came home looking more troubled than was usual for him. She knew that something was wrong.

'I saw my brother today,' he said when she asked what was bothering him. 'I saw my brother Taiye at St Pancras.'

Ever since Kate, his wife, Nehushta's mother, died he had changed beyond recognition. A grey peninsula had evolved overnight on the tousled wilderness of his balding head. His eyes peeked out of their sockets, lonely and devoid of purpose, like lights shining into a great void revealing nothing but the darkness ahead.

2

He was almost fully functional during weekdays. His workload as an immigration lawyer kept him busy and with no time to brood. ('The *difficult* we do immediately,' he comforted a client facing imminent deportation. 'But,' he added, 'the *impossible* takes time to accomplish.')

3

Weekends though, he came home reeking of alcohol and all bandaged up.

'I've been walking into things,' he would say to his daughter, 'lamp-posts — and pubs mostly,' before passing out on the sofa.

4

When he came home that night looking agitated, Nehushta poured him a glass of whiskey and watched him hurriedly knock it back.

'I saw my brother today,' he said, holding out his glass for another tipple.

'Your twin-brother died twenty years ago,' she said gently.

'I know he died twenty years ago,' Ossie said. 'Why else would I be so shaken?'

5

It happened that evening on his way home from work. He was under a twelve-month ban for drink-driving so he'd left his car at home. He was waiting at a bus stop near his office in King's Cross when the incident happened. A black cab drove past. And there, in the back seat, sat his brother, Taiye. Ossie blinked, not quite believing it. He shut his eyes and opened them again: and there he was, Taiye, riding in the back of a London black cab. He ran after the cab, waving wildly. The cab driver looked startled, but not nearly as startled as Ossie's brother who looked positively alarmed. The cab turned a corner and disappeared.

6

'I swear, Nehushta. It was him, it was Taiye.'

She said nothing. She knew that nothing she said would make him change his mind. And it seemed churlish to point out to him that not only had his brother died two decades ago, but that he'd died back in Lagos, without having ever left the shores of Nigeria, let alone come to London.

7

'I poured him another drink,' Nehushta told Dada years later when he and she were lovers, 'and said to him something I'd once heard him say to one of his friends, "You cannot stop the birds of sorrow from flying over your head but you can prevent them from building nests in your beard."'

'What did he say?'

She smiled. 'He keeled over and fell asleep.'

8

Nehushta pulled off her father's shoes and half-carried, half-dragged him to his bedroom. She took off his tie and tucked him into bed. He was snoring loudly when she turned off the light and shut his bedroom door behind her.

9

As his daughter switched off the light and shut his bedroom door after her that night, Ossie Jones drifted from a deep, drunken sleep into a dream in which he was completely sober and in his car driving down a strange, liminal highway that stretched from a nebulous tunnel at the soles of his feet, past the toll-gates of his soul, where he was stopped, even his passport checked, and into the boundless openness of the universe.

10

On the glittering and limpid stopwatch known as his destiny, which he may or may not have had on his wrist that night, it was around two in the morning. A vicious wind colluding with heavy rains transformed the journey into a blind, non-stop flight on a treacherously endless highway.

11

On the car stereo, the jazz flutist Eric Dolphy abducted the Billie Holiday song, *God Bless the Child*, into a scorched emptiness at the back of his mind. It emerged bittersweet from his flute, a private cry, leaping and bounding and soaring into a silence that rang in the ear like the moment into which a scream dies and hope is born.

12

It was Ossie's favourite instrumental rendition of *God Bless the Child*. And whenever he heard it, he felt a glow, a joy within him. It took him back to long-forgotten moments in the backwoods of his past. It took him back to the days of his youth when he first arrived in England in search of what his parents in Lagos called 'the Golden Fleece'. His grandmother, who didn't want him to go away, and whose mind was sharper than a mosquito's bite and probably as lethal, took great pleasure in pretending to be senile. She wondered aloud why, under heaven, or beneath the sea, or in the firmaments of hell, anybody would want to possess a flea, golden or not.

God Bless the Child took him back to the first time he'd met Nehushta's mother, Kate, at a Jazz club in West London. Kate was a nurse at the time, and he'd barely started his law degree at the London School of Economics. The grand plan back home was that he would take his first degree, go to Oxford for a doctorate, and then go back to Nigeria to start a law firm. That was the script, as written and choreographed by his father. As it turned out, his father died, a civil war broke out in Nigeria and his graduation at LSE was delayed for three years because his scholarship was cut off during his final year. Nothing, but nothing, went according to plan. The only constant in his life, the one person who stood by him when all else were jumping ship, was Kate. They were both in their twenties, and it was the Swinging Sixties. When she took him home to meet her parents in Sevenoaks, her father was quite charming to him and then phoned her the following day to ask her if this was her way of getting back at him for he-knew-not-what? Her mother seemed singularly incapable of duplicity and made it clear to him that she had her fingers crossed about his relationship with her daughter. With time, she grew to like him and they became good friends. He got married to Kate five years after they started seeing each other. Two years later, Nehushta came calling from the land of the Unborn. Twelve years later, Kate went for a routine medical check-up. A week later, on the first day of spring, she went back for the results. She came out of the doctor's surgery counting her life in months.

Up until that point in his life, Ossie's relationship with the concept of God had been casual and indiffer-ent. It wasn't so much that he didn't believe in God: he just wasn't in a hurry to meet him.

13

Ossie panicked after Kate was diagnosed with cancer. After they'd run the gauntlet of mainstream specialists and alternative gurus, after they'd travelled to America to meet the 'world's leading authority' on that species of cancer, and after they'd been to Brazil and back, and not found satisfaction, Ossie panicked and turned to

God. When Kate passed away, peacefully, less than a year later, Ossie was still at the back of the queue to see God. As he knelt beside Kate's bed in the hospital, crying bitterly over her still warm body, a voice inside him screamed out, 'Why, God, why?' and he finally found himself at the top of the queue. God, invisible as always, spoke to him. 'It was Lucifer,' said the voice of God, gently. Infuriated that God seemed to be passing the buck, Ossie stopped crying and looked up, spoiling for a fight. He saw his daughter holding on to his hand. He got off his knees, reined in the tears, and began to play father to his child.

14

In Ossie's dream, his car suddenly stopped. He got out of the car, into the rain and opened the bonnet. He messed about with a few plugs but soon gave up after the stalled engine raised his hopes three times and three times dashed them against the hard shoulder.

15

He proceeded to attempt to cadge a lift. Several cars went by without stopping, but finally, after he'd been standing in the rain for a quarter of an hour, drenched and shivering, salvation appeared in the distance. Its headlights grew bigger and brighter and then it screeched to a halt within inches of him. He was caught between the headlights, sepulchral, crowned with a halo of self-pity. The lights dimmed to reveal a limousine. The driver leaned out and shouted, 'Hurry up!' It was a boy's voice, the voice of a young man. For a nanosecond he stood frozen to the spot, paralysed by a certain dissonance, an inexplicable feeling of foreboding that took possession of him. 'Hey, mister!' the boy said impatiently. Ossie hurried to the slightly open door, taking off his topcoat as he got into the car.

16

'You can put that in the back of the car,' the boy said. Ossie looked at him. The boy was, as Ossie had guessed from his voice, quite young; no older than sixteen. He was chewing gum, loudly, busily. The boy offered him one. Ossie shook his head. The boy shrugged and threw it into his mouth. 'I said put that in the back,' he said again looking at Ossie's coat. Ossie folded it and put it on the floor.

'You are a vagrant,' the boy declared. Then before Ossie could respond, the boy asked the question to which he had already provided an answer: 'What are you – a vagrant?'

His tone indicated that he wasn't in the least bit interested in a reply. And he wasn't. Before Ossie could de-freeze his tongue, and offer a suitable reply, the boy went on.

'You look tired,' the boy said. Then, like before, he provided the question to an answer. 'Are you tired?'

'I am quite tired,' Ossie said.

'You have a family.'

'Yes—'

'Do you have a family?'

'Yes, I—' Ossie began.

'Wife?'

'I'm – I lost my wife.'

'What about kids? You have kids. Do you have kids?'

'Yes, one.'

'Boy?'

'No.'

'Girl?'

'Yes, she's—'

'I knew it had to be a boy or a girl.'

Ossie turned to look at him. The boy's eyes were firmly fixed on the road ahead.

'Sorry,' he said. 'I'm a bit hyper tonight.' He reached into the glove compartment and pulled out a pack of cigarettes. He struggled briefly to open the pack and take a cigarette. The road was wet and slippery. Ossie reached out and took the pack from him. He pulled out what appeared to be a filterless cigarette and handed it to the boy and helped him light it.

'Your car broke down.'

'What?' Ossie said.

'Did your car break down?'

'Yes.'

'Smoke?'

'No,' Ossie said, 'I don't smoke.' He cleared his throat. 'Where were you coming from?'

'Here and there,' the boy said, with the sighing equivalent of a yawn. 'You?'

'London.'

'Where's that?'

Ossie couldn't be bothered to respond. But the silence that followed bothered him. 'Where are you going?' he asked.

The boy shrugged again. 'Nowhere in particular,' he said.

'Never heard of it.'

The boy turned to look at him. 'What?'

'I've never heard of Nowhere-in-particular. Is it a city or a village?' Ossie laughed. He laughed because he realized that it was a weak joke, and he knew himself well enough to know that he only made jokes like that when running on empty, when he'd lost his bearings and was on the verge of panic.

'I'm just strolling,' the boy said earnestly.

'To Nowhere-in-particular?'

'Yes,' the boy said.

'Nowheresville. That's a strange place to be going at this hour of the night.'

'I'm just taking a stroll,' the boy said mildly. He reached out into the glove compartment and fetched another cigarette.

17

'I'm Apha,' the boy said, lighting the cigarette. 'You are—?'

'Jones. Ossie Jones.'

'Tell me a joke, Ossie,' Apha said. 'Do you know any jokes?'

'A joke?' His stomach rumbled loudly. 'Worms,' he explained.

'Worms?' Apha looked mystified.

'My stomach,' Ossie said.

Apha looked even more perplexed.

'I haven't heard a joke in ... months,' he said, moving on. 'Don't you know any jokes? My dad used to tell me jokes.'

Ossie grabbed at the straw. 'Your dad? Is this his car?'

'Yes,' Apha said. 'His name's Max.' He paused before asking, 'Did I tell you my dad's name?'

Ossie was tempted to answer in the negative, just to see what effect this might have on the boy. But before he could do so an odd, gravelly sound escaped from Apha's throat. At first, Ossie thought it was the beginning of bad smoker's cough. Then he realized that it was the sound of laughter. Apha was laughing. 'Of course,' he said, laughing with all his body, 'of course! I told you my dad's name. I did tell you his name, didn't I? Didn't I?' He stopped laughing. A faraway look came into his eyes. 'My mind is playing tricks on me,' he said in a small, childish voice.

'Are you all right?' Ossie asked. 'Do you want me to drive?'

'Oh, I'm fine,' Apha said. 'I'm perfectly all right.'

18

'This missionary goes to Africa,' said Ossie. 'He goes to this village and sets about saving souls. One of his first converts is a farmer. The missionary baptizes him, teaches him to read the Bible and makes him a Catholic. He tells him that, next to Sunday, Friday is the most important day in the week of a Catholic. No eating meat on Fridays, he says, and no telling lies either. Or it's hell and damnation. One Friday, several months after the conversion took place, the priest pays a surprise visit on his new convert. Lo and behold, the man is tucking into a huge bowl of buffalo soup! The priest is furious! "Peter," he says, "didn't I tell you that eating meat on Friday is a mortal sin?" "Yes, Father," says Peter, licking his fingers, "but I'm not eating meat. This is fish." "You call that fish!" exclaims the priest. "Not only are you eating meat on a Friday, you are also telling a lie!" "I'm telling you, Father, it's not meat, it's fish," says Peter. The priest picks up a chunk from the buffalo soup and holds it up to the light. "Tell me, Peter," he says, "how you arrived at the conclusion that this piece of red meat is in fact fish." "Easy," says Peter, "I just poured a bowl of water over it and called it fish. Just like you did when you baptized me from Mtata to Peter!"'

There was a long silence after Ossie finished telling the joke.

Perhaps, Ossie thought despairingly, when Apha still hadn't responded moments later, perhaps Apha was a vegetarian, and was deeply offended by jokes about meat.

19

Apha was no vegetarian, and he wasn't offended by jokes about meat. 'Where,' he asked after a long and pensive silence, 'is Africa?'

20

It did at that point cross Ossie's mind that he should get out of the car and wait in the rain for another vehicle to come along. But the thought occurred to him only fleetingly, and then it disappeared, unheeded and sulking, to the silence of memory.

21

'Tell me about your dad,' Ossie said.

'What do you want to know about him?' Apha asked.

'I don't know – anything. For instance, what does he do? And how's he doing?'

'He is an academic,' Apha said, 'his field is jurisprudence. How's he doing? Not too well is how he's doing.'

'What a coincidence, I'm a lawyer myself.'

'Well, good for you.' The words, coming from Apha, had the violence of an expletive.

Ossie rearranged his facial muscles into a smile grafted upon a grimace. 'How do you mean he's not doing too well?'

'Are you sure you want to hear this?'

No, I don't, he said in his mind, but I'm trapped with you in this car and I'd better act sharp.

'Of course I do,' he said hastily, as his eyes briefly strayed from the road and bored into him.

'It all started two months ago. He came home from the university with this woman he introduced as his graduate assistant. Her name was Lizzie. She was helping him carry out research on a new book he was writing.'

'Where was your mother?'

'She left home a year ago. After paying him a surprise visit one afternoon at his office and finding him flatting with one of his students.'

'You mean, flirting, trying to seduce?'

'Flatting. The student was flat on her back and he was flat on her stomach.'

'I see, *in flagrante delicto*.'

'What's that?'

'Caught red-handed,' Ossie explained.

'Oh,' Apha said.

22

'When he brought Lizzie back to the house that night, I'd assumed she would stay for a drink and then go away. You know, just go away. But I was wrong. I went to bed. When I woke up the following morning, she was in the kitchen making herself a coffee. A week later, she was still with us. A month later—'

'Did this bother you?' Ossie asked.

'Only all the time.'

'I see. Did you discuss this with your dad?'

'I was going to.'

'But you didn't.'

'I was going to. Last night. They were out when I came home. They got back around midnight, as I was about to go to bed. They both came into my room, flushed with champagne and announced they were getting engaged.'

'And how did you react?'

'I shot them both.'

23

This isn't happening, Ossie prayed in his mind, it's only a dream.

'You what?'

'Point-blank,' Apha said, 'with this—'

He reached under his seat and pulled out a pistol. He tossed it on to Ossie's lap.

'Oh God,' was all Ossie could think to say. 'Oh God.'

'Would you like to see them?' Apha asked politely.

'What?'

'Would you like to see their bodies? They're in the boot.'

'No,' said Ossie, slowly picking up the gun and realizing, as he picked it up, that in all his forty years and more, he had never held a gun before.

This was not quite true. In the parallel world, outside of this dream he was dreaming, he'd once handled a gun in a firearm store in Wyoming. But in his dream, this memory eluded him.

Before he could compose and articulate a response to Apha's offer to show him the bodies, Apha had cut the engine and was already stepping out of the car.

'Come on,' he said.

Ossie slowly followed him.

24

But as Apha made to open the boot, powerful lights suddenly transformed the night into stark, rain-serrated daylight. There were police cars, and helicopters, everywhere.

'Drop your weapon,' said a voice through a megaphone, 'you are completely surrounded.'

25

Ossie looked around him, not quite comprehending the great calamity that was about to befall him.

26

'Drop your weapon,' barked the megaphone voice, 'repeat: drop your weapon.'

It was only then that he realized that the order was being addressed at him. He looked at his hand and found he was still holding the pistol. He let it drop to the ground. A while later, he was slammed violently against the car and a pair of handcuffs was slapped on to his wrists. He looked around and saw Apha bursting into tears.

'He could've killed me!' Apha screamed angrily, hysterically, at the officers. 'I triggered the alarm ages ago, why did it take you so long to get here?'

'What's this, Apha?' Ossie asked, only slightly panicking. 'What's happening here?'

'They're in the boot,' said Apha. 'He put them in the boot.'

'Who?' asked an officer.

'My dad and his girlfriend,' cried Apha. 'This man killed my dad and his girlfriend!'

'Officer—' Ossie began.

The policeman opened the boot, looked inside briefly, and retched. He turned to Ossie and pulled out a tiny digital recorder.

'What's your name, sir?' he asked Ossie.

'Jones,' said Ossie. 'Ossie Jones. Officer—'

'Address?'

'1205 Battersea Park Gardens, London. Officer—'

'Occupation?'

He told him.

The officer brought the recorder closer to his mouth.

'Ossie Jones,' he said, 'you are under arrest on suspicion of murder. It is my duty to inform you that anything you say will be taken down and might be used in evidence.'

27

It was at this point, as he lay in handcuffs and pressed against the car, that Ossie realized that his dream was in fact a nightmare.

28

He had no recollection of the journey to the police station. He tried to wake up from the dream (for he did know it was a dream) by pinching himself, and banging his head against everything in sight (including the face of one of the officers between whom he was sandwiched in the back of the patrol car – the unfortunate constable, who had never arrested a murderer before, ended up with a nose the shape of a stepped-on tomato). For Ossie, it was all to no avail. And his dream would not let go of him.

29

At the police station, he watched as officers engaged in a series of long telephone conversations and mini-conferences that were punctuated by frequent and increasingly bemused glances at him. One of them finally came over to him.

'I need a phone,' said Ossie. 'I'd like to speak to my lawyer.'

The man studied him and said nothing. He seemed quite amused.

'Officer, I *demand* to speak to my lawyer.'

'All right,' said the officer, 'what's his number?'

'Can I have a phone, please?'

The detective dragged a phone over to Ossie's table. 'Go ahead,' he said, 'call your lawyer, Mr Jones.'

Ossie brought out his electronic organizer, a birthday gift from Nehushta.

'This is all a terrible mistake,' he said as he dialled his lawyer. 'You'll see, that boy was lying through his teeth. He told me that he killed his father and the woman.'

The room had gone completely silent.

Ossie listened as the individual digits of the number he had dialled clicked into place. The police station was on an old, analogue telephone exchange. He waited for it to ring. He waited and waited. Then he dialled again. And then again. He got the same result each time: a robot which said to him, 'The number you've dialled has not been recognized. Please try again.' Ossie tried to look unfazed. 'I've written down the wrong number,' he assured the police detectives, 'do you mind if I phone my daughter? She'll know the number. He's her godfather.' They simply stood there looking at him as if he'd just dropped in from another planet. He dialled his home and again the robot informed him that the number he had dialled had not been recognized. He thought he detected a note of amusement in the robot's voice. 'This is absurd,' Ossie said with deep irritation. A pronounced panic, low-level, from the soles of his feet to the nape of his neck, was beginning to take possession of him. He dialled every single number in his organizer, and several that he knew by heart; he dialled new friends and old acquaintances, Kate's mother and his local pub; he even dialled an old friend who was no longer a friend (they fell out over something petty and inconsequential twenty years back and hadn't spoken to each other since). He phoned every one and everywhere, and got the same results: either the number was no longer available or it had not been recognized.

At last the phone was wrestled from his hands and taken away.

30

'Let's start all over again,' said the police detective. 'Who are you?'

'I've already told you,' said Ossie. 'You've got to believe me.'

The detective pulled up a chair and sat directly across from Ossie. 'Mr Jones — may I call you that? — you simply don't exist, Mr Jones. There isn't an Ossie Jones. Not a lawyer, or a plumber, or even a vagrant or a cat. We've checked up every piece of information you've given us, and every last bit is a piece of fiction. There are no records of the driving licence that you gave us, no records of the drink-drive misdemeanour that you claim to have been charged with. You have been showering us with a confection of lies, Ossie Jones, and we are beginning to get very, very cross with you. Now, for the last time: who are you and why did you kill Max Wren and Lizzie Johnston?'

Ossie had stopped listening from the moment the

detective pulled up the chair to sit down. His panic was so intense that his heart stopped beating once and he had to be resuscitated. The kiss of life also had the effect of oxygenating his brain. He jumped up and burst out laughing. 'Officer,' he said, 'I know why those lines are dead, why you think I don't exist. It's because you don't exist! I'm in a dream. I'm dreaming!'

They led him to the cells and threw him in with a comatose man who had been brought in for being drunken and disorderly.

31

Ossie's trial was a quick affair. He did not help his case, or endear himself to the judge and the jury by insisting, at every opportunity, that they didn't exist and that he was in a dream from which, *Ha! Ha!*, he'd soon wake up. He insisted on being addressed as Jones even after the most exhaustive investigation by the police revealed that no such person existed. And since the address at which he claimed to live did not exist either, he was referred to throughout the trial as 'Ossie Jones of no fixed address'. He dismissed his lawyer after she advised him to plead guilty on grounds of diminished responsibility. He guessed, quite rightly, that she genuinely believed he was insane.

Apha was brought in to take the stand. And he described how, on the night of the murders, he had been sitting in his bedroom, reading a book on bots for his Artificial Intelligence exams, when he heard a noise in the living room. At first he said, he thought it was his father and his father's girlfriend, Lizzie, coming back from their dinner date. However, something made him uneasy and he decided to go and check. He went downstairs to the living room, and there he was, the man he now knew as Ossie Jones, pulling out a cabinet of drawers and rifling through them. Apha hid underneath the staircase. A few minutes later, his father and Lizzie came back. His father came in first, followed by Lizzie. When Ossie turned round to face them, he had a gun in his hand. He wasn't violent at first, Apha said, until he asked Max, his father, for money. Max told Ossie that if he didn't leave immediately he would call the police. Ossie, Apha claimed, laughed and said, 'Be my guest, call the police.'

The public prosecutor, listening intently, rearranged her baldness as if it were a wig.

32

His father, Apha continued, moved towards the telephone. And it was as he started to dial that Ossie shot him in the face. Lizzie screamed, turned to run away, and he shot her too. In the back. He emptied a few more shots into them. That was when he, Apha, rushed to an open window and jumped out. He landed on the front lawn of the house and was about to try to make a dash for the neighbours' when he saw that his dad's car was parked outside, and not in the garage. He had obviously been aiming to go out again that night. He'd had an extra set of keys made the year before after he kept losing them. By a stroke of luck, Apha had the extra pair on him that night. He ran to the car, got inside and was about to start the engine when he felt a touch of steel on the back of his neck. He turned round to see Ossie Jones leering at him. Ossie told him to get out. He obeyed. He told Apha to follow him back into the house. Apha did so. Then he told Apha that the two of them, together with the bodies of Max and Lizzie were about to go on a trip. He made Apha drag the bodies out to the car, one after the other, and then he threw them into the boot. Then he pushed Apha into the car, jumped in beside Apha and told him to drive. Apha asked him where to, and he said just drive.

33

'Answer yes or no. Have you reached a verdict in the case of the Crown versus Ossie Jones?'

'Yes.'

'How do you find the defendant: guilty or not guilty?'

'Guilty.'

And thus Ossie Jones was found guilty of two murders he didn't commit and sentenced to life imprisonment. He was told that a life sentence in the land of dreams (which, he found out, had no name) meant precisely that: life without possibility of parole.

34

Ossie was in a haze. He sat in his cell clawing at his mind, his sagged jaws cupped in the sweat-moistened palms of his hands.

35

His only respite was sleep. When he slept, in this land of dreams, he had no dreams, no nightmares. And sleep was not as he had known it. In the land of dreams, sleep was what happened to you when your mind drifted from wakefulness into a mist of hebetude. You could take a walk, turn on the radio and listen to the weather report, meet up with friends, make love, go to the cinema, play football, or even read the newspaper. You could physically do all these things and more even as you slept.

36

Ossie's choice of things to do was of course circumscribed by the confines of his cell.

37

At the beginning, he held on to his old habits and would lie down in the ritual of going to bed. He would lie on the floor for several hours, inert, covered in a blanket of dullness, aware that although he was completely asleep, he was in fact awake.

38

But he learnt fast. A fellow prisoner guided him to wisdom, a man named Johni, who was serving the second of three life sentences for homicidal crimes of passion he committed during a previous lifetime. Johni was thirty when he began the first sentence, and, fortunately for him, died five years later. He was born again twenty years after that. Two prison warders were waiting outside the maternity ward when his new mother gave birth to him. He was barely five minutes old when he was handed to them in a nice little pram, which he had had the prescience to buy during the last few weeks of his previous existence. It had been kept for him by one of the prison warders who kept it in the most pristine condition after Johni died and until Johni was born again. The warder cleaned it every year in spring, oiled its wheels and sometimes pushed it to the park and back, just to keep it in shape. As it turned out, this same warder was selected by Providence to sire Johni into the world again.

39

Johni was not as lucky during his second life sentence as he had been during the first. It was his plan to die as soon as possible so that he could return, at the earliest opportunity, to serve his third sentence and have the whole thing done with. But Death crossed the road to avoid him whenever it saw him coming. One day, during the morning stroll that all inmates were allowed to have, he caught sight of Death in the loop of a knot hanging from an improvized rope that another prisoner had just used to commit suicide in a secluded spot behind the prison gym. Johni was the first person on the spot and he arrived as Death, who looked rather bored and overworked, was pulling the suicide into the world beyond the land of dreams. Johni, seizing the opportunity, ran up to Death and begged him to take him along.

It was not the fact that Death told him to 'piss off' that provoked Johni. Nor was it the fact that Death, who was in the habit of chain-smoking long cigars to control his short-temper, called him a buffoon. What infuriated Johni and triggered his own even more volatile temper was that Death started laughing at him. Johni's first punch, when it landed, not only knocked Death to the ground, it drew blood from Death's nose. Such was the ferocity of the punch, such its thunderous intensity, that the steel gridirons in the visitors' hall, which was on the other side of the prison, shook. And the suicide was frightened back to life. Death managed (heaven knows how) to get on his feet. Then he broke into a run. According to those who witnessed the event, those whom he sprinted past, it was as if Death had seen a ghost. Johni, who was a nice guy at heart but a complete psychopath from head-to-toe, bounded after Death. He chased Death up and down the prison threatening to strangle him if Death did not take his life. Luckily for Death, the governor's office was open, and he found sanctuary there.

40

Death was traumatized by the incident, and so angry and humiliated, that for twenty years he boycotted the prison and the town in which the prison was situated.

41

During those years not a single prisoner died, not a single inhabitant of the town contracted a terminal disease, and not a single being aged a day older than they were from the day Johni assaulted and chased Death across the prison.

42

Those years during which Death inflicted a moratorium on the inmates of the prison and the inhabitants of the town did not prove to be the happiest for them. On the contrary, despondency hung like fog in deepest winter over the prison walls and misery jutted down like icicles from every lamp-post on the streets of the town.

This was the reason why: the people found out that in the absence of Death, Life couldn't exist. In other words, when Johni chased Death out of the town, he inadvertently also chased Life to the city limits and bolted the gates. The ethical, not to mention the logistical, questions raised by this state of affairs were complex and unassailable. To the outside world, it was impossible to say whether the inhabitants of this one particular town in the land of dreams were dead or alive. It was said that they were neither dead nor alive. Something had to be done.

43

The outside world convened a conference of philosophers, mathematicians, physicists, metaphysicians, poets and moralists. It was held in an ancient auditorium in the hinterlands of the land of dreams.

44

No minutes of the proceedings were kept; no records of the presentations, or notes of the discussions that took place at the Conference of Life and Death, as that meeting came to be known, exist.

45

This has led some historians to extrapolate that no such conference ever did take place. They point out that it was the custom in those days to make no contradistinction between a truth and a lie. Truth, in those days, was believed to be fluid. A truth was merely a lie whose time had come; conversely, a lie was simply a truth being conceived. It might have been claimed that the Conference of Life and Death took place, not because it did take place, but because it was believed that everything that could happen would happen eventually, and that the Conference of Life and Death, if it had yet to happen, would happen sooner or later.

46

One day, exactly twenty years after Johni chased Death into the governor's office and was restrained by six warders and a chaplain, a great conflagration broke out in the eastern wing of the prison. No one knew how it started, who started it (if indeed somebody had started it) or precisely when it started. The only thing that was beyond dispute was this, that by the time the fire services managed to put out the fire several hours later, the eastern wing of the prison had been reduced to smouldering ash.

Five inmates took advantage of the distraction to briefly re-acquaint themselves with the outside world, and ten people (eight prisoners, a warder and a man who had been visiting) died.

Death had returned as dramatically as he had left. The celebrations, all over the land of dreams, went on for weeks.

47

The confrontation between Johni and Death took place when Johni was eighteen. By the time Ossie Jones experienced his oneiric transfiguration and found himself serving a life sentence in a prison in the land of dreams, the Duel-with-Death was so far back in the past it had already begun to take the status of legend. Ossie was watching a soccer game one afternoon a few months into his sentence, the first time he had ventured out of his self-imposed isolation, when a voice from behind him said, 'You're Ossie.' He turned round to see Johni, who looked to be forty but was actually approaching seventy-five.

'I hear you've been having problems sleeping,' said Johni, after introducing himself as one of the longest-serving members of the prison community.

'Not the longest-serving of course,' he hastened to add. 'I've only been inside for seventy-five years, give or take a few hours. Some have been here longer. Chew over there, for instance—' He pointed at one of the footballers who was in the process of scoring a goal. 'Chew is ninety-eight, and doing the third of seven life sentences.' He made a noise of horror. 'Imagine that. Seven life-sentences. I only got three, and I'm well into the second. Who am I to complain?' he said, bringing out a pack of cigarettes.

'Smoke?' Johni lit a cigarette.

Ossie shook his head.

Johni made smoke rings that frittered into the ether but kept coming back like a bad memory.

48

Then Johni asked him, 'What's this I hear about sleeping problems?'

This was news to Ossie. 'I don't know what you're talking about,' he said.

'Come on,' said Johni with a smile, 'you know how it is in this place. Nothing, not even your innermost secrets, goes unnoticed.'

'As far as I know, I have not been experiencing any problems sleeping,' Ossie said. Then, to change the subject, he asked Johni what he was in for.

Johni looked at him with a vague curiosity. 'What planet are you from?'

It was a rhetorical question but Ossie didn't know that. 'I'm from the planet Earth,' he said earnestly and was about to launch into another protestation of his innocence when Johni burst out laughing.

'You're all right,' said Johni laughing. His laugh was loud, long and deep. And his eyes watered when he laughed.

' "I'm from the planet Earth," ' he mimicked Ossie. 'You're crazy, but I like that.' He continued, 'I don't know where you've lived all your life, Ossie, but every school kid knows that the only crime punishable with a custodial sentence is murder. Every single man-child in this prison is here because they slit someone's throat, or shot someone, or spiked someone's drink with cyanide. You're not seriously telling me you didn't know that?'

'I didn't,' said Ossie truthfully.

'Then, my friend, I don't know why they sent you here. Normally they send people like you to the nut-house.'

'My lawyer wanted them to do that, but I sacked her,' said Ossie.

'Why?'

'Because I'm not mad.' Ossie paused, and then he added, 'I think.'

'Who did you kill?'

'Nobody,' said Ossie.

49

'Who did you kill?' Ossie asked Johni.

Johni had no reservations telling Ossie that he was inside for mass murder.

'You're a serial killer?' Ossie glared benevolently at him.

Johni shook his head emphatically, looking disgusted. 'Not a serial killer. A mass murderer. There's a distinction. I went on a spree in a supermarket. Killed three people, including my girlfriend. My lawyers claimed it was a crime of passion. They found out that she'd been messing about with one of the guys I shot so they said it was a crime of passion.'

Ossie didn't regard himself as a murderer, and he hadn't quite got used to hanging out with murderers. 'You mean to say it wasn't – a crime of passion?' He looked shocked.

Johni vigorously shook his head. 'No. I didn't even know she was out shopping when I went into the place.'

Ossie wanted to end the conversation there and then, but he felt he might offend his new-found friend if he didn't pursue the matter further.

'Why did you do it then?'

Johni considered the question for a while before

answering. 'I was just acting out a joke,' he said quietly, no longer laughing.

'Excuse me?' Ossie asked, choking.

'What does an armed-man do in a supermarket?'

'I don't know,' said Ossie.

'He goes on a shooting-spree!' And Johni doubled with laughter once more. 'You think I'm crazy, don't you?'

Suddenly, the soccer game seemed irresistible. Ossie excused himself and went on the field.

50

In his father's youth, Johni told Ossie the next time they met on the soccer field, his father had been a lively, hell-raising miner (with a heart the size of an Olympic stadium. Legend had it that in those days, he had a smile that was so bright and warm, people dried their laundry under it).

That was in the days of his youth. In middle age, and no longer a miner, his laughing eyes stopped laughing, and became sadder than an eternity of winters. He was a decent man, Johni's father, but he was cursed with thinking and plagued by his mind, so he drank all the time.

It came as no surprise to those who knew him that on the day his wife went into labour with their fifth child, he was spotted on the roof sipping homemade gin, ninety per cent proof. When his wife broke water, and the baby's head emerged, the man was heard to remark to his drinking companions that if it wasn't a girl this time (all the previous four were boys), he would walk out on her. He would later swear, upon the stars and the comets in the sky, that he had only meant it as a joke. Unfortunately, the visitor from the land of the unborn did not think much of the joke.

That visitor, who would come to be known as Johni, withdrew back into his mother's womb, and vowed not to come out until the day his father died. According to the older neighbours – who knew about these things – when the baby returned to the land of the unborn, he explained to the authorities there that he did go to the world but found that it was closed. In this way, he got them to extend his residence-permit for another nine months.

He remained there until the day when, in the land of the living, his father-elect downed a cocktail of gin, guilt and orange juice, climbed to the top of a hill in the Valley of a Million Hills, and missed a foothold.

That was when Johni ended his protest. He came out from his mother's womb, grinning from ear to ear at precisely the moment his father went screaming to the final full stop of his short, uneventful, and generally unhappy tenancy in the land of the living.

'Some said it was suicide,' Johni said to Ossie. 'Others said that for contemplating suicide he was killed by the demiurges. And others said that his death was nature's way of telling him to give up drinking. The truth will never be known. So' – he looked Ossie in the eye – 'that's why I turned out the way I did. Damaged. Beyond repair.'

Ossie thought he had missed part of the story. 'I'm not sure I . . . understand,' he said.

'Don't you see?' cried Johni. 'I felt rejected by my father. I felt he didn't love me.'

They watched Chew take a penalty kick.

51

'About your sleeping problem—' Johni began.

'I don't have a sleeping problem,' Ossie said.

'What do you do when you're nodding off at night?'

'I lay out my bed on the floor and go to sleep.'

'And what do you do while sleeping?'

'Take a guess, Johni.'

'This is serious.'

'I sleep!' said Ossie in exasperation. 'What do you do when you're sleeping?'

'I study,' said Johni. 'Sometimes I do a few hundred press-ups, but mostly I read books. It's the best time to read, while you're sleeping. Your mind is at its most focussed, its most retentive.'

And that was how Ossie learnt to read while sleeping.

52

One morning fifteen years later, Ossie sat thinking about Johni (who had been dead for five years) and dwelling on Nehushta (whose face haunted his waking moments and his dream-bereft nights; her face was bright and wildly intoxicating like a child's face when it smiles the first time). He reflected about the degree in Astronomy, which he'd recently acquired by correspondence, of course, and through studying while asleep. A prison warder came banging on his cell door.

'You have a visitor,' said the warder, as he led him to the governor's office.

'Sign this, please,' said the governor, a taciturn man, handing him some forms.

'What is it?'

'Your release papers,' said the prison governor. 'You're free.'

Ossie froze. He felt ill, rather than elated. He groped around and found a chair.

'Where am I supposed to go?' he asked loudly. But the question really was to himself.

'Sign the forms, please,' said the governor. 'Someone's waiting for you outside.'

Slowly, hand shaking, he signed the form. He went back to his cell, packed all his 'earthly' possessions into a bag improvised from one of his shirts, and walked, like a man to the gallows, towards freedom.

53

As he walked across the soccer pitch, which separated the bulk of the prison from the main gate, he watched an ambulance pull in. It stopped beside him. Two prison warders stepped out of the back of the ambulance. They were carrying a pram between them. It looked familiar.

He went over and peeped into the pram. There was a baby inside, a toothless, beautiful child barely a few hours old.

'Johni!' Ossie cried. 'You're back!' Trembling with excitement, he turned to the warders. 'It's Johni, isn't it? Johni-the-mass-murderer?'

They nodded rather glumly.

'It's Johni all right,' said one of them. 'But the bugger's gone and come back as a lass.'

Little Johni, fast asleep in her pram, was blissfully unaware of the juridi-cosmogonic dissonance which her arrival was unleashing on the penal system. Ossie promised to come back and see her sometime.

Outside the prison, there was a car waiting for him. Again, his equanimity was violated by a visitation of *déjà vu*. A man stepped out of the car. Ossie's heart stammered when he saw him. It was Apha. Although he was now in his early thirties, he had aged little from that terrifying night fifteen years ago.

'Get in,' Apha said, holding the door open for him.

Ossie did not attempt to get into the car.

'What are you doing here?' he asked.

'I came to apologize,' Apha said, 'and to take you wherever you wish to go.'

'I have no wish to go anywhere with you,' he said.

'Please.'

'I have nowhere to go.'

Apha took Ossie's bag and threw it in the back of the car. Then he led him into the car.

'I confessed,' he said. 'I told them everything – what really happened. That's why you've been set free.'

Ossie didn't know what to say.

'Why did you do it? Why did you frame me?'

They were driving away from the prison.

'Because you were there,' Apha said simply. 'I'm sorry.'

'Why are you still free then?'

'I'm out on bail. My trial begins next week.'

He sat quietly, his misery in the cup of his hands.

'Tell me what you're thinking,' Apha pleaded.

'I have nowhere to go,' he said.

'Why don't you come to my place? Please say yes. It's the least I can do.'

So he said yes. He wanted to ask him why, after all this time, he had chosen to come forward now. He knew Apha would have an answer, an explanation. He chose not to ask him. He knew that if he did, the residual sediments of hate that had settled at the bottom of his heart might dissolve and slip away. He didn't want that. Not just yet.

'Remember Lucy?'

'Lucy?' He had no idea who Lucy was.

'The Public Prosecutor,' Apha explained.

54

Ah, the balding prosecutor.

55

'We got married, and—' Apha pulled out a photo album from a bag by his feet. 'We've got two beautiful kids, Eva and Gabriel.'

Ossie glanced uninterestedly at the kids who, he had to admit, looked no worse and no better than their parents.

'They know all about you,' Apha said.

56

In the land of dreams, objects disappeared the moment you looked away. They travelled backwards and for-wards in time and space, to part-time duties in distant planets or brief assignations in parallel universes. They reappeared just as soon as you turned round or opened your eyes to implicate them in your existence.

The last thing Ossie saw before he fell asleep were Apha's eyes, open wide as if to a fleeting moment of pleasure or a sudden, unexpected terror.

57

He emerged into consciousness. A strange yet familiar smell, disturbing yet comforting, invaded his nostrils and sent self-replicating, self-cancelling signals of joy and sadness to his brain. A radio was in the vicinity. It was tuned to an extraterrestrial station. A strange noise – music – accosted him.

58

His ears stepped tentatively into the room.

59

Ossie opened his eyes and looked around him. There was a woman in the room. She sat in a chair by the bed, reading a book whose title he could not decipher. It was Virginia Woolf's *To the Lighthouse*.

'Excuse me,' he said to the woman, 'where am I?'

The woman looked up.

Ossie saw Kate, his dead wife, looking at him with an expression of unmitigated joy and consternation. Ossie realized, with relief, that he was dead and in heaven.

Nehushta started screaming and crying at the same time.

'Father! Father!'

60

Ossie Jones awoke from a coma that had lasted fifteen years.

THE PICNIC

1

Within four weeks of emerging from the coma (or, as he liked to call it, his 'subterranean odyssey'), Ossie was given a clean bill of health by the astounded doctors at the West London hospital where, to all outward appearances, he had vegetated for fifteen years. An intrepid news-hound who worked for a local newspaper, which was owned by a national newspaper, brought the story to her editor's attention.

Within days of Ossie's awakening, he was on the front page of every newspaper, and headlined every bulletin on radio and TV.

Ossie, his every syllable resonating with relief and gratitude, was 'simply glad to be back' and not troubled in the least by the paparazzi invasion. 'They will get bored with us soon enough,' he assured his twenty-eight-year-old daughter as a BBC television crew departed, to be replaced by the CNN pack. He was wrong: to the degree that the strange and unknowable nightmare from which he had emerged had made him a more patient, perhaps even a wiser person, it appeared to have endowed him with an almost child-like naivety. The newspapermen and television crews were insatiable, insurmountable and from every corner of the world. So were the celebrities and movie stars, and the pop icons. Everybody who was anybody found their way to his bedside and said cheers with him for the cameras.

The perennial debate about euthanasia came again to the fore. It became the intellectual-wallpaper of choice, and inspired an infinite permutation of sound bites, bon mots and repartees. A panel of medical experts, social scientists, politicians and members of the public was invited to a live television debate on the topic. It began cosily enough, with each side presenting arguments, counter-arguments, and a generous offering of Trojan horses. Soon enough, an intemperate tongue sashayed into a fragile ego. The collision transformed the well-intentioned communal chinwag into a collective fit that ended with everyone dissing everyone else and accusing them of being 'politically correct'.

Ossie watched the debate from his hospital bed. 'Politically Correct? What does it mean?' he asked his daughter.

'It's the great bogeyman from the Pandora's Box of the New World Order,' she informed him.

'Come again?' Ossie asked.

'Pandora's Box,' said Nehushta. ' "The first woman," ' she quoted, ' "brought with her from heaven; when she opened it, out of curiosity, all escaped into the world, except Hope." '

Ossie nodded patiently, but that was not his question. His question, which suddenly didn't matter, was,

'What's the New World Order?' His face furrowed in deep thought. He studied his daughter's face. 'You're very angry, aren't you?'

'No,' she said, shaking her head.

'You're angry with me and your mother.'

'No,' she said.

'You felt abandoned.'

Her answer this time agreed with the movement of her head. 'Yes,' she said in a whisper.

'I'm sorry, Nehushta,' he said, holding her to his chest. 'I'm really sorry.'

They held each other, crying loudly, and messily, together.

2

Helen, his late wife Kate's mother, came to see Ossie. Bill, her husband, had died the year before, and she now lived on her own in a little cottage in a village near Sevenoaks. It was from Helen that he found out what had happened, parallel to his other journey, that night fifteen years ago. She and Bill were getting ready to retire for the night, she said, when the phone rang.

'It was Nesh,' she said, shutting her eyes, as if invoking the moment into the present tense. 'She didn't say a word at first. But I knew, from her breathing, that it couldn't be anyone else. I said, "Darling Nesh, is that you?"' Nesh was her pet name for Nehushta. 'She said, "yes". "Is everything all right, darling?"

'She said, "It's Dad, he . . ." and she started crying.

'I said – I knew something was wrong – I said, "What's wrong . . . is he there?"

'She said, "He's . . . here . . . on the floor. He fell out of bed. I heard him, I was in the bathroom. He made a real racket. I ran into his bedroom, and there he was, flat out on the floor, with a big gash on his head."

'She tried to wake you, to resuscitate you, but couldn't. So, she phoned for an ambulance. The ambulance arrived while she was still talking to me. She was very brave that night. I felt very proud of her.'

Helen and Bill drove down to London to the hospital Ossie had been taken to. It was well past midnight when they arrived. Nehushta was seated on a bench in the corridor that led to the wards. The nurses had tried to get her to go to bed in a room in the hospital but she had refused. She took them to the doctors, who were in the emergency room, where Ossie was laid out on a respiratory machine. His head was heavily bandaged. Several tubular devices attached to a brain-scanning machine protruded from the bandage. He was immobile, frozen nearly, and there was scant visible sign that he was alive. The life-saving devices humming and flickering all around only served to underline the picture of mortification that lay before them. That was the good news.

The doctors took them outside and told them the bad news. They told them that (as far as they could tell), when he fell out of bed, he banged his head against a sharp object (which, on investigation, turned out to be a corkscrew), which tore into his skull and grazed a nerve. The trauma of the foreign invasion proved to be too much for the nerve. It died (or committed suicide) and consequently shut down sections of Ossie's nervous system. It was a rare condition normally associated with horrific car crashes, but there they were, Ossie had it, and he was in a coma. There was little they, the doctors, could do. People had been known to come out of it, but proportionate to those who never did, the possibility was, at best, infinitesimal.

At the time, nothing the doctors said made much sense. But after the first week had gone by, and the first month rolled into the first year, it became quite clear that the initial prognosis was right: Ossie had plunged into a deep coma.

They sold Ossie's house in Battersea and put the money in a trust fund for Nehushta, or for him, if he ever came out of the coma. Nehushta moved in with them. Initially, they visited him every fortnight. Then, as Nehushta grew older and her studies became more demanding, they went once a month.

'Didn't the question of switching off the life-support ever crop up?' Ossie wanted to know.

It did. Quite a number of times. But right from the very start, Helen and Bill had decided that this was a decision only Nehushta could make, and they didn't feel it should be put to her before she reached twenty-one. And that was what they told the doctors. The doctors were quite happy to respect the family's wishes. But not so the hospital authorities, who took the matter to court. The case went on for four years.

The courts decided that Ossie's condition should be reassessed in another three years, which, by no coincidence, would be Nehushta's twenty-first birthday.

On her birthday, Nehushta decided to spend the day with him. She invited a couple of her close friends from university. Bill and Helen and several members of the hospital staff were also invited.

It was a very small and very quiet party. After she'd blown out the candles and they were eating the cake, Nehushta decided she wanted to play some music. Helen was against the idea, because she reasoned, not only would they be disturbing Ossie, they would be disturbing other patients.

'Disturb Ossie?' Nehushta screamed, completely losing her rag. 'Of course I want to disturb him! I want him to wake up, dammit!' It was quite a scene. As granddaughter and grandmother were screaming at each other, with Nehushta in tears and Helen getting very upset, one of Nehushta's college friends suddenly took a sharp intake of breath.

'What's the matter?' someone asked her.

She looked ashen, her face weighed down in shock. 'He moved his hand!' she said, pointing at Ossie. 'I swear! I saw him move his hand!' The room went deathly quiet. They all turned round and looked at him. His left arm, which had been lying inert by his side, and which had not moved an inch unaided in nearly seven years, was hanging loose on the side of the bed.

'Oh my God,' cried one of the nurses.

It never happened again. But after that, the

hospital authorities carefully avoided any mention of euthanasia.

3

The first thing Ossie did when he was discharged from the hospital was visit Kate's tomb. It was the first time he felt the need to beg the cameras to allow him and his daughter some time to themselves. The cameramen, bearing him no malice, granted him the moratorium.

The visit, to the lush cemetery in the direction of Dover, took place on one of those bright summer days when scantily clad natives of London, vying with tourists wearing baseball caps and sombreros, unleash themselves on the outdoors with the singular and inexorable ferocity of an act of nature.

'It's quite busy in here today, isn't it?' Nehushta remarked at the cemetery as they made their way through a throng of visitors, and across a serrated mass of headstones, to her mother's resting-place. At each gravestone that they went by, they saw families armed with hampers packed with food, crockery and cutlery, and sitting on mats spread out on the grass among the yew trees. The cemetery resembled not so much a cemetery as a park minus the roller-blades. The pic-nickers were happy and contemplative, sad and effer-vescent, preoccupied and extroverted, ageless and young. The variegated colours of their moods, the diaphanous texture of their souls and the slow-roasting fire of their angst illuminated even those hidden secrets of the cemetery that lay beyond the gaze of the sun.

One or two shouted out greetings to Ossie and Nehushta.

'Nice people, aren't they?' Nehushta said. She waved.

As they went further into the graveyard, these picnics of the dead became rare, and soon there were none. A sombre and elegiac mood, crystallizing into an inarticulate celebration of silence, came over them.

Presently they arrived at their destination, a simple headstone inscribed with Kate's name and, as she had wanted, mentioning her daughter's name and her husband's, now intertwined between the crawling plants which Helen and Nehushta had planted and nurtured over the years. They lay down the flowers they had brought, pruned the plants with a pair of shears Nehushta had brought along and sat down to talk to Kate. They tossed a coin to decide who would go first. Nehushta won.

She made herself comfortable and proceeded to tell Kate that she had dumped Russell.

'Russell?' echoed Ossie.

'My ex-lover,' Nehushta said, barely pausing as she poured a bottle of her mother's favourite wine into three glasses, one of which she placed beside the flowers. 'Cheers, Mum. Welcome back, Dad.'

Ossie raised his glass, 'To Kate – you're alive because every time we breathe, you breathe in us. And to you, my daughter, my beautiful daughter, and to us all.'

They clicked their glasses against Kate's glass.

'How long were you with Russell?' he asked, trying to sound oh-so-casual.

'Six months,' she said, laughing. 'Don't worry, Mum knew all about it.'

'And why are you no longer together?'

'Because we split up, Dad. Shut up, will you. I'm trying to have a conversation with Mum.'

And she went on to tell Kate why she finally decided, actually only a week before Dad suddenly rose from the dead (oops, Mum! I mean, from his coma), to tell Russell that Russell was a self-obsessed, self-aggrandizing prat and would he kindly shut the door after him, please. (Why? Did you say why, Mum? His idea of a conversation was this. HIM: 'Stop interrupting me. Hush. Did I interrupt you when you were speaking?' ME: 'I haven't spoken yet.' HIM: 'Exactly. As I was saying . . .' And, Mum, Mum! I know I told you this last time, but I have to, I just have to tell you again: was he crap in bed? Was he! His idea of foreplay was ten minutes of begging . . .!')

Ossie listened, feeling guilty almost, as if he were eavesdropping on an intimate conversation between two people he didn't know as well as he used to. This was his somewhat belated realization that the thirteen-year-old girl he had left behind had become this altogether grown-up woman sitting beside him on the grass. As she went on talking to her mother, another penny dropped, and he felt an immense relief, a deep gratitude to her: he realized that this prattle with her mother about her private life was actually, indirectly, a conversation with him. She was bringing him into her world, telling him, this is who I've become, this is who I am.

He leaned over and kissed her on both cheeks. He felt sad, and happy in his sadness.

It was soon his turn to speak to Kate. He started out by telling her how much he missed her, how much they both missed her. He told her about that night fifteen years ago, how he had drifted into sleep. Admittedly, he said, he had had a couple of drinks, but only a couple. ('More than a couple, Dad,' Nehushta interjected.) All right, more than a couple, but not so much that he wouldn't know what he was doing—

'You did pass out, Dad.'

'Did I?'

'Well, you didn't *pass out* pass out, you fell asleep on the sofa in the living room and I had to help you up to your room.'

'Oh.'

He told Kate how he found himself in a dream – he knew it was a dream, he said – and how, when his car in the dream stalled, a boy who introduced himself as Apha pulled up in another car and offered him a lift.

As he continued his story, which Nehushta was hearing for the first time, he saw her blink with what at first he thought was disbelief. But he saw, as he continued the story, that it wasn't that. It was simply terror. He saw her eyes saving the questions for another time.

They stayed till late afternoon, then they bade Kate farewell. As they were about to leave, Nehushta suddenly remembered something.

'Oh, by the way, Mum, we're going on a trip across Europe.'

'Who are "we"?' Ossie asked, surprised.

'My friend and me. His name is . . . on the ticket.' She pulled out two tickets from her bag and gave them to him. He didn't bother checking for the destinations, his eyes went straight to the names. And there they were: Nehushta's name and his name. His immediate response, after smiling within, was to ask her where the money for the trip had come from.

'I took out my savings,' she said.

'You did what? We've got some serious talking to do, young lady.'

'I was planning on going anyway – with Russell.'

'Would you have had to pay for him as well?'

'No. But he hadn't been lying in a coma for fifteen years. And he sure wasn't my father. Listen, Dad, I want you to come along. I think it will be good for us.'

'When did you make this incontestable decision to co-opt me into this?'

'When you asked me the other day what the New World Order was. Really, Dad, you don't have to go if you don't want to.' She was starting to sulk.

They walked in silence for a few seconds. Then he said under his breath, 'Try stopping me.' She swung round and (although she was far taller than he) jumped into his arms.

'On one condition, though,' he said.

'What?'

'I pay for everything else: food, hotels—'

'It's a deal.'

They shook hands on it.

'Thanks, Nehushta,' he said.

She pinched his hand. They walked back to Nehushta's car, barely noticing that the necropolitan picnics had evaporated. As they were heading back to Brixton, where she lived, she turned to him. 'Seriously, Dad, what you told Mum – all that stuff about "the land of dreams" . . .'

'Every word, every last punctuation mark,' he said.

'Jeeze,' she whistled. 'Why didn't you tell the doctors when you woke up?'

'It did cross my mind, but it seemed so incredulous – even to me – I thought it was better not to. I didn't want them starting to worry about the state of my mind.'

'Have you been . . . back there since you . . . returned?'

'No. In any case, I seem to have lost the capacity to dream.'

'No one loses the capacity to dream. Hasn't it bothered you that it could happen again?'

He shook his head. 'I don't think it would. I *know* it wouldn't. Don't ask me how I know. I just do.'

And he did. He hadn't suffered a moment of insomnia since he woke up.

They were now in Brixton. She drove round Market Row and Granville Arcade a couple of times before she spotted a free parking slot. She eased into it.

'Can't you park on your street?'

'I can. But we've got some runnings to do here.'

'Was that my hearing or was it your diction?'

'What?'

'Runnings.'

'Follow me, Dad.'

She led him across the road into a barbing salon.

'Oh, I see. I need a haircut, is that it?'

'You're catching on real fast, Dad.'

'Any other coming-of-age rituals lined up for me today?'

She consulted an imaginary Filofax. 'Five-thirty, circumcision. Five-thirty-five, make you an offer you can't refuse: either we get you a new wardrobe or you turn yourself in at the nearest tailor's.'

'Thanks for consulting me, Miss Jones.'

'You're welcome, Mister Jones.'

'Is that what it's really called?' he asked reading out the name of the barber's. 'Beards Trimmed While You Wait.'

'Yes.'

'Not bad. Can I have a coffee afterwards? I'm dying for a coffee.'

'Bah Humbug is just round the corner. We'll go there.'

'Bah Humbug? What's that?'

'Restaurant and coffee bar.'

'Beards Trimmed While You Wait and now Bah Humbug. I think I'm beginning to like your neck of the woods. When you were a kid, your mum and I used to come shopping here on Saturdays. In those days, that was all it had going for it: the market. A friend of ours at the time had a saying, "The only good thing to come out of Brixton is the bus passing through it."'

'That's a bit strong,' said Nehushta, taking an intense dislike to her father's friend, as if the man was there, right then, in person.

'He was a man of strong opinions,' said Ossie, smiling. 'And it was a long time ago.'

They went into Beards.

4

As it happened, Dada was in Bah Humbug that afternoon. It was situated in the crypt of an old church opposite the Fridge nightclub. The tetchy clock-tower that stared stolidly at the high street, from the town hall across the road, had just struck quarter past five (he didn't hear it strike, but his memory insisted that he did), when they walked in: a black man in his late fifties or early sixties, West African sepia, and a woman in her mid-twenties, whose mother, if the man was the woman's father, and it was Dada's guess she was his daughter, was almost certainly white.

Dada was having a drink with Midé, the bookseller who moonlighted as a stand-up comedian. And as was usual whenever they met, he had a new joke, a brand new joke, which Dada just couldn't wait to hear.

Actually, he could wait. But it was much easier to sit through Midé's jokes than to try explaining to him why you didn't, just didn't, want to listen to a joke just then. His response, if you told him you weren't up to it, would be along the lines of, 'Is it because I'm

black?' which was guaranteed, and intended, to pro-
voke an intense and long row. That afternoon, Dada
was neither in the mood for a joke, nor was he in the
mood for a row. So, he opted for the joke.

'This guy goes to see a doctor,' Midé said. '"Doctor," he says, "please help me: I just can't stop nicking
things." "Here," says the doctor handing him a prescription, "two of those three times a day for a week.
That should do it. If not – get me a VCR."'

Midé smiled broadly. 'What do you think?'

Dada placed his hands on the table, one on top of
the other, trying to figure out the best way to say what
he was about to say.

'What?' Midé asked suspiciously.

'Well,' Dada began, 'I think it's . . . funny, no,
witty, short, precise, brilliant, original, engaging—'

'Stop pissing on me and—'

'I'm not—'

' – telling me it's rain.'

'What I'm driving at—'

'Stop driving. You haven't got a driving licence.'

'Look, Midé, what I'm trying to say is – I think
it's a good joke but – and this is completely irrelevant—'

'If it's irrelevant, don't tell me.'

'Well, it's irrelevant in a . . . germane sort of way.'

'You are so full of shit.'

'Midé,' he said finally, 'I've heard that joke
before.'

His mild irritation turned into pure fury:

'Not from me, you haven't.'

'Precisely what I'm saying,' Dada said. 'You said it was a new joke.'

He knew the moment he said it that he'd just bought himself a one-way ticket to the gulag called Midé's Bad Books. He closed his eyes and stilled himself for the explosion. But something extraordinary happened: the explosion never came. He opened his eyes thinking Midé had stormed off. He hadn't. Even more intriguing: he'd simply lost interest in him.

Dada turned and followed Midé's thoughts, which seemed to have wandered with his eyes across the room.

That was when he first set eyes on her. She came in first. And he, the father figure, wearing a sharp, natty haircut with which he seemed ill at ease, appeared moments later. Before Dada noticed her face, which seemed to emerge, haunting and dimly seen, as from the fading brilliance of a majestic sunset; or her hair, which danced about her head, down to her ears, like stars in pursuit of a wanderer moon; before he heard her voice, or caught a whiff of the aroma of her silence; before he saw her smile, or calibrated the cadences of her laughter, he was drawn to, and ensnared by her eyes: they were big and glistened, a combustible shade of red. In them, he later told the Heckler, who kept saying, easy, Dada, easy, he saw gypsy-clouds sojourning on a dewy-faced mountain crest, he saw strange landscapes with iridescent plants that did not yet have names, he saw rainbows burnished with the broad-strokes of an indifferent genius. He saw the birds of the air, and the beasts of the land, and the inhabitants of the sea. He saw planets that did not exist in time, space or the imagination. He saw imaginary beings that had been spoken into existence. He witnessed a night that was illuminated, not by stars, but by a luminous constellation of hopes.

As he looked into those eyes, in that brief, immutable moment, they turned into a deep turbulent pool. And he saw, before his own eyes, the whole bar drowning in it.

He shook his head, feeling dizzy. He was plunged into a feverish mist. In the mist he saw, rising from the illusion of an illusion, the smoky-eyed jinni of the spliff he'd had before breakfast; he swam in the rapid streams of the beers he'd had after lunch, and he noticed the bloodstained remains of the wine he'd shared with Midé. He realized, with a relief bordering on epiphany, that he was utterly and unrelentingly drunk.

In a hushed voice, he said to Midé, 'She *is* beautiful, isn't she?'

Midé muttered, '*Who?*'

He realized that Midé had merely been trying to catch the waiter's eye. Midé succeeded after much persistence. Then he saw her. 'Her?' His lips curled derisively. 'Don't you read the papers? Has your TV been repossessed?'

'Talk to me, Midé. What are you talking about?'

He heard her order a double espresso for her father and a cappuccino for herself. They pulled up stools by the bar and sat down.

'First off,' said Midé, 'I want you to know that I

understand why you're so envious of me, my creativ-
ity—'

'Midé—'

'You're like a performance poet: all performance,
no poetry. And to compensate for that obovoid vacuity
that used to house your brain, you've become bitter,
twisted and, let's face it, vindictive. You define success
by the tally of genuinely talented, hardworking people
you're able to drag down into that gutter only you
know so well.'

'Come on, Midé,' Dada said mildly. 'I only said I'd
heard the joke somewhere before.'

He couldn't be bothered to take the bait.

The waiter came to their table. Midé slapped some
coins into the man's hand. 'That's the tip,' he said.
Then, pointedly not looking at Dada, he said, 'He's
getting the bill.' And with that he got up and left.
Dada shook his head. This was the third time he'd
been out drinking with Midé when he'd conveniently
stormed off in a huff, just before the bill arrived.

Dada looked up at the bar. She was whispering
something into the old man's ears. They burst into
laughter. He liked the sound of her laughter.

He paid the bill and added an extra tip. 'Listen,
mate,' he said to the waiter, 'know those two at the
bar?'

He nodded. 'His name's Ossie Jones. There's been
nothing but him in the papers and on telly for the past
four weeks. He's the bloke who came out of a fifteen-
year coma, completely recovered.'

'Really?' Dada wished now that he still read the

papers. And that he hadn't pawned his television set. 'And who is she?'

'His daughter.'

'I don't suppose you know her name, address and telephone number.'

The waiter laughed so much he had to hold on to a chair.

'You're joking, aren't you?'

Dada shook his head.

The waiter's face hardened. 'Listen, mate, if you want her name and number why don't you go and ask her yourself?'

'Brilliant suggestion,' Dada said. 'I shall do just that.'

But as he staggered to his feet, he made two discoveries: that his bladder was bursting, and that Ossie Jones and his daughter had left. Dada swung round on his heels and headed for the gents.

He had no recollections of what he did as he stood by the urinal. He thought he peed. But he couldn't say for certain that he did.

He remembered coming out and searching in vain for the door that led back to the bar. He stumbled about in the treacherous labyrinth of the crypt, walking through stone walls, bumping into thin air and holding on to empty darkness. Finally, with the eyes of a cat, he came across a door. It was a rickety, wooden affair, ravaged by time and abused by human neglect.

He did not notice the sign, which read: 'WARNING: THIS DOOR IS ALARMED'. When he tried to push it open, the door – which was already bruised, trauma-tized and suffering from low self-esteem – cowered before him and nearly flew off its hinges. Dada, almost as startled as the door, almost jumped out of his skin.

The phone rang. Slowly, he opened his eyes. It was morning and he was in his flat and on his sofa bed. He woke up and broke out in a sweat.

5

Head first, hands flailing, Dada had fallen in love with a woman in a dream.

THE PLAY

1

The two hoods, one named Noir, the other named Blanc, were seated in what looked like a Porsche convertible in an open field some place unspecified. Monsieur Noir and Monsieur Blanc were dressed in black — dark suits, dark shoes and dark glasses. Even the watches on their wrists had black straps. These, combined with the dark, shimmering guns lying on the dashboard endowed the two men with a mildly sinister, discombobulating presence.

M. Noir chewed gum loudly and incessantly, smoked cigars and (for reasons completely lost on Ossie, who was watching them from the rock-hard seats of a pub theatre on a stupendously hot summer evening), scratched and, or, re-arranged his testicles every few seconds. M. Blanc had more or less the same habits, although he didn't scratch his balls nearly so often. It seemed that the crucial difference between these two characters in *Cool Killers* was that where M. Noir was broody and quiet, M. Blanc was broodier and twice as quiet.

Presently, M. Noir checked his watch. Then he looked into the far distance. On this occasion, and in this theatre, the far distance was situated exactly where Ossie was seated.

'Why is he looking at me?' Ossie asked Nehushta after checking to see that the only things behind him were the walls.

'He's not looking at you, Dad,' Nehushta explained patiently, knowing he was merely being mischievous. 'He's looking at a house across the field.'

M. Noir scratched his scrotum and took a long drag at his cigar. 'He always gets up at six on the dot, without fail,' he said to M. Blanc, exhaling a cloud of smoke that had the appearance of a bubble. Ossie looked again. It was a bubble. The smoke followed later.

M. Blanc, whose clean-shaven head was drenched in sweat, now introduced a facial tic into his lexicon of mannerisms. 'Supposing today he doesn't?' he asked his mate, twitching his face.

'Then we go in there and ask him why not,' said M. Noir, taking a long drag. 'Sit back, all right? Relax. I've done this . . . so long as things go strictly according to plan, and you're alert when you have to improvise, it's a piece of cake.'

'What's his story?'

'What's his story? I don't know what his story is.' M. Noir rearranged his balls. 'I don't know that he even has a story.' Pause. 'Even if he did have a story do I wanna hear it? No, thank you, I don't wanna hear it. Do you wanna hear it? No. You don't wanna hear it, believe me, you do *not* wanna hear that man's story. Why not? Because if you did then what the fuck are you doing in this army?'

'Ah, they are soldiers,' whispered Ossie.

'No, they're not,' Nehushta snapped.

But M. Noir was still insisting that he was in the army. 'What the fuck are you doing in any army, for that matter?' he barked at his partner.

Ossie nudged his daughter. 'He said it again.'

Nehushta ignored him.

M. Noir was on a roll. 'What I'm saying is, and this is a *for instance*, if you're a soldier and you're sent to war, you're sent there to hurt the enemy, to subvert, to kill him, to eliminate him, to make dust of his dreams. Your bullet is the full stop at the end of his life, *period*. That's what you're sent there to do. Simple arithmetic: subtract him from himself.'

A light came on behind Ossie's head.

'See,' said M. Noir. 'Six on the dot. That's what I call being reliable. D'you know Woody Allen?'

'Are you kidding?' said M. Blanc. 'I went to school with him.'

'Go on, brag about it. In one of his films Woody says—'

'Woody, ay?'

'He says, "Crime pays. The hours are good, you travel a lot." Guess what: he's right. Did you see *Crimes and Misdemeanours*?'

'Yeah,' said M. Blanc. 'My favourite actor was the dog. Are you crazy, or what, M. Noir? We're on the verge of sending someone to that great place in the sky and all you can find to talk about is Woody—'

'"The great place in the sky." And you say *I'm*

being flippant. You don't like Woody Allen, is that what you're saying?'

'That's not what I said,' said M. Blanc heatedly.

'I'll tell you why you don't like him—'

'I never said I didn't like him!'

' – It's because you're scared of emotions—'

'Fuck you.'

'It's true. You're afraid of expressing yourself.'

'I can't believe I'm hearing this.'

'That's how come you never scored with Emma.'

'Some relationships go beyond the mere physical. There's also something called a spiritual dimension.'

'Yeah? What goes on there: virtual copulation?'

'You know, I feel kinda sorry for guys like you.'

'Guys like me! Who was the wise guy who kept sending flowers to Emma for a whole year and didn't even get to see her underwear – in the laundry – let alone—'

'Hey, let's set the records straight once and for all: I never sent her any flowers. I never sent her a single flower.'

'You didn't?' M. Noir scratched his balls. Then he looked incredulous.

'I fucking didn't,' M. Blanc insisted.

'Not even on Val's Day?' M. Noir looked incredulous. Then he scratched his balls.

Ossie was beginning to feel sorry for the man's balls, and for the concept of incredulity.

'Val's Day my ass.'

'You see what I'm saying? It comes back to: you're

afraid of your emotions, the lover in you. That's why you don't like Woody Allen.'

'If shagging your own daughter—'

'She wasn't his daughter—'

'If shagging your own daughter is what you call being romantic, then, yes, I'm not romantic.'

'She wasn't his daughter and, anyway, don't use words like that: shagging. I hate it when people use words like that. What happened to good old "love-making" . . . making love. Shagging. Shafted. "They copulated." Fuckingchrist, what are "they": train carriages? "He had carnal knowledge of her." Where? On a butcher's slab? I mean, fuckingchrist, I'd rather you said, "They fucked." At least that's unpretentious, and it captures something of the essence of—' M. Noir broke into a grin. 'I'm a New Man.'

'Oh, really? Haven't you heard he never existed?'

'Bollocks. Take it from me, it's the only way to get laid these days. And look, it's all right to do that Woody Allen-is-a-prick thing. Just don't lay it on too thick.'

'For the hundredth time, I'm telling you, Woody bloody Allen is—' M. Blanc stopped in mid-speech. Something he'd seen behind Ossie had made him stop.

'He's coming out,' he said to M. Noir.

M. Noir picked up his gun from the dashboard. He did a few things to the gun, such as loading it with a clip of bullets, cleaning the muzzle, and the like. Then he stepped out of the car, pseudo-masturbated one last time (one for the road), and spat out the chewing gum. Then he walked purposefully in Ossie's direction, which also happened to be the general direction of the exit. The stage lights faded to black, and the house lights came on.

2

Downstairs, in the queue at the pub, Nehushta seemed to know everybody and everybody knew her. She introduced him to the director, a thin little man with a receding hairline and a whit of hair that segued into a ponytail. He wore a distracted look and mumbled something incoherent to Ossie before wandering off. The writer appeared moments later, the very picture of glum. He looked tortured and was hugging a pint of lager. He too ambled on after spitting a macedoine of constricted vowels, strangulated consonants, cryptic silences and elliptical pauses, seasoned with saliva, into Ossie's beer.

'Why do they both look like they've been kicked by a mule?' Ossie asked.

'They have that effect on each other whenever they are forced to breathe in the same air,' Nehushta explained. 'They fell out during auditions. Ron, the playwright, hates the actors – basically because he had other actors in mind for the parts, but Hugh turned down every single one of them – and Ron absolutely, absolutely loathes Hugh's interpretation of his text. He boycotted the rehearsals.'

Ossie gave her his mug and went in search of the loo. When he came out a few minutes later, as he turned into the short corridor that led to the bar, he heard shouting. He turned round to see the playwright, further down the corridor, in the opposite direction, screaming at the director.

'Is that what you think?' the playwright was screaming. 'You think I'm fucking with you, you think I'm fucking with you, you thinking I'm fucking with you, is that what you think? Is that what you think? I'm fucking with you? You think I'm fucking with you, I ain't fucking with you, I don't fuck with nobody, I ain't fucking with you, I ain't fucking with you, you ain't fuck, fucking you fucking, fuck, I ain't fucking with you, fucking fuck, fuck, fuck, fuck.'

The playwright quietened after the expectoration. Then, close to tears, he said, 'That's the line. I just quoted it to you. Where did it go? What did you do with it?'

The director explained ('Calm down, Ron, it's only the second preview') that they'd found, during rehearsals, that the line just didn't work so they left it out.

'Didn't work? Didn't work!' screamed the playwright. Now he looked like he'd stepped on a nail. 'The best fucking line in the first act and you tell me it didn't work? You know what? I'm going to phone my agent first thing on Monday. I want that line reinstated or I want my name taken off.'

'Come on, Ron, it's just a couple of fucks!'

'Seven fucks and twelve fuckings actually, you fucking philistine.'

Ossie left them to it and went back to the bar.

Nehushta handed his beer back to him.

'Now, Dad, tell me, how did the play really strike you?'

'How did it strike me?'

'Honestly.'

'Honestly and frankly?'

'Frankly and honestly.'

'Well,' said Ossie, 'if you mean, did I like it, the answer is, yes I did and no I didn't.'

'How do you mean and how don't you?' she retorted.

Ossie, grinning: 'I liked the way it said what it was saying, but I didn't think it was saying anything or that it had anything to say. But I believe in freedom of speech. I believe that everybody who has absolutely nothing to say has the God-given, inalienable right to say it. I think that in writing this play, the writer was merely exercising that fundamental human right and should neither be applauded nor chastised for doing so. On the other hand, I think it's quite brazen of him to require me to pay him to do so.'

'Except you didn't have to pay, Dad. You came in on a comp.'

'True. But beside the point. I ran into the playwright and the director just now by the loo and almost yielded to the temptation to ask them an important question.'

'Which is?'

'I wanted to know which of them was responsible for luring my daughter, undoubtedly under false pretences, into this psychotic farce—'

'It might be psychotic, Dad, but it certainly isn't a farce.'

'How do you cope with it?'

'It's not always like this. And it's not as bad as it seems.'

'That's what the Invisible Man said.'

'What?'

'"I'm not as bad as I look." Seriously though, the best thing this production has going for it is, I think, the stage design. It achieves a certain classical symmetry, a coherence of vision that is lacking in the rest of the show.'

'Flattery, and a travelcard, will get you anywhere, Dad. But I still have to disagree with you. I do think Ron has something to say, and that it does come across in the play.'

'And what is this thing that he has to say?'

'It's not so much a message as a mood that he's trying to put across. I think he's trying to capture the zeitgeist. It's about art imitating art imitating art.'

'Aha. Now I understand, that's why the characters all sound like characters trying to sound like characters trying to sound like Humphrey Bogart.'

'Since you've been away, Dad, not only has the world been getting *meta* and *meta*, every *post-* has been postponed.'

'And how is the postal system coping with the deluge?'

'Admirably well, all things considered' – then, deliberately stepping on his foot – 'oops, sorry, Dad.'

'What I'm saying – and I will not be intimidated,

lady – is this: what happened to the chronicling of recognizable, three-dimensional, plain simple folk?' he asked. 'What happened to Joe-and-Jane-on-the-street? What happened to art imitating and celebrating, or interrogating and re-imagining reality?'

'Hit men *do* exist, Dad.'

'Yes, but how many does your playwright know?'

'The vision behind *Cool Killers* is grounded in a reality,' she argued. 'It's just a different kind of reality. Joe-and-Jane-on-the-street are nowhere to be found in Ron's world for the simple reason that he doesn't know them. He was too busy in his parents' attic watching tapes he'd rented from the local video store.'

'Now, isn't that sad?'

She lit a cigarette. 'What's sad about it?'

'He needs to go out more, get a proper job, hang out with Mickey Mouse and Bonnie and Clyde a little less often. As you would say, he needs to get a life.'

She checked the time. 'We should leave soon.' They were going to have a meal at a restaurant in the West End.

'But first,' she said, 'I'd like you to meet the cast.'

'Can't we just wag our tongues at them on our way out?'

The actors were seated at a table by the door.

'Come on, Dad.'

'What should I say if they asked me what I thought of the play?'

'The truth, Dad, tell them the truth.'

'The truth? The unvarnished truth?'

'The truth – varnished, unvarnished, in whatever

shape or form. As long as it's the truth.' She paused.
'But under no circumstance must you tell them you
didn't like their performance.'

'You are asking me to lie?'

'I'm asking you to show some sensitivity.'

'But I didn't like their performance.'

'Then don't mention their performance.'

'I can't just *not* mention their performance.'

'Get in there first. Ask them what *they* thought of
their performance.'

'And if they thought they were brilliant?'

'Tell them you absolutely adored their suits.'

'I positively hated their suits.'

'If it's only a matter of verbs, Dad, you're welcome
to borrow mine.'

'You can keep your verbs. I'm perfectly happy with
mine.'

'Come on, Dad! Tell them . . . I don't know . . .
tell them certain aspects of the play reminded you of a
play by Harold Pinter. Then *talk* about Harold Pinter.'

'I don't know much about Harold Pinter.'

'Use your nous, Dad.'

'"Meta" and now "nous"! Where do you get these
strange words from?'

'Come on now. It should be relatively painless. You
are a lawyer after all.'

'That is a very wicked thing to say.'

3

In the end, they decided not to go to the restaurant in Soho. They opted instead to pick up number 13, number 22, number 8 and number 40a from her favourite Chinese take-away, a joint called Wok Away on Acre Lane. They picked up a six-pack of beer at Lickle Mo's, a Jamaican off-licence ('Please Do Not Ask For Credit, As A Smack In The Face Often Offends'), and headed back to her flat on Brixton Hill. During the drive, they talked about their trek across Europe, on which they would commence in a few weeks, and about a trip across Africa that he had mooted to her. They would start in southern Africa around Christmas and make their way early in the New Year by air, land and water to the western end of the continent. They talked about the paparazzi who, mercifully, had discovered or invented a new obsession and left them alone. And about the tabloid newspapers that had offered him a staggering amount of money for his story. He had declined the offers, opting instead for a publishing contract with a company whose back-list included many of his favourite authors. He might agree a serialization deal when he'd written the book. In the meantime, he would rather not tie himself to any newspaper deal.

Nehushta's grandmother, Helen, had been astute in her handling of the proceeds from the sale of his Battersea house so he had enough in the bank to start house hunting as soon as his travelling was over.

His old law firm was still in business. He'd paid

them a visit the other day at the same offices in St Pancras. There had been many changes in personnel, the faces were younger, but two of the top partners from his time were still around and they had told him he could have his old job back whenever he was ready.

He told Nehushta about the Astronomy degree he had acquired during his incarceration. They were driving back from the take-away when he mentioned it. She pulled up the car by the side of the road, and stared at him, her hands gripping the steering wheel.

'You got a degree in Astronomy?'

'Yes,' he said. 'But it's all gone since I woke up. I can't seem to remember a damn thing about it.'

He could see that she was worried.

'Dad.' Her tone was tentative and, therefore, ominous. 'I've been thinking about—'

'My story about the land of dreams?'

'Yes.' She laughed nervously. 'I thought you were about to say you knew this was coming.'

'How can I when I don't know what's coming?' This was a lie. He had known it was coming. He had been waiting for it ever since he told her the story.

She ran her hands through her hair. 'Don't you think you should talk to someone about it?'

'I have. I've talked to you about it.'

'Yes. But I mean someone . . . unbiased . . . some-one objective.'

'You mean a shrink?'

'Well, yes, a psychologist.'

'Better still, I could see an oneiroscopist.'

'What's that?'

'An interpreter of dreams. How about that?'

'You're being hostile, Dad.'

'All right, I'm sorry. I know you've had it on your mind ever since I told you—'

'It isn't that I don't—'

'And I know this is difficult for you, having to tell me to go see a shrink. And you know what? I'll phone the General Practitioner first thing tomorrow.'

'Dad, I'm not . . . You will? Promise?'

'Promise. I'll phone him and tell him I want to see a psychologist.'

She kissed and embraced him.

'I love you, Dad.'

They drove in silence for a few minutes. As she swung into her street, she turned to him.

'You do know I believe you, don't you?'

'I do.'

'You do?'

'If I didn't think you could handle it, I wouldn't have mentioned it when we went to see your mum. I mentioned it because I knew I could rely on you to give me the benefit of the doubt.'

'Thanks, Dad.'

'I should be thanking you.'

She pulled the car into the nearest free parking slot. They got out and began to walk back towards her flat, a few blocks away.

'You remember that incident Granny talked about when she came to see you at the hospital?'

He stopped. 'The one about your birthday party?'

'Yes.'

'Don't tell me you set it up?'

She nodded.

'Oh my God.'

'I'd known about the court case, and I knew that if something tangible didn't happen after my twenty-first that they would probably . . .' She couldn't bring herself to say the words. 'So I hatched up this plan with my closest mates at university.'

'Oh my God,' he said again. 'How can I thank you?'

'Let me think,' she said, then she decided. 'Just thank you will do.'

'Thank you, angel,' he said.

It was one of those summer evenings when at nine o'clock the sun was still abroad, loitering with coruscating intent. A police car, siren blasting, flashed past. Two old ladies, Nehushta's neighbours, taking their poodles on a late walk up and down the street, went past them on the pavement.

'I trim 'im meself,' said one of the ladies looking dotingly at her dog.

'How do you trim 'im?' the other one inquired.

'With scissors,' replied her friend.

In an easy silence, Ossie and Nehushta walked to the flat arm-in-arm.

4

'It's like the man who sets out to show his friends that his cat is a genius,' Ossie was saying. ' "What is ten minus ten?" he asks the cat. The cat looks sullenly at him. "See? She said nothing," the man says triumphantly.'

Yet again that night they were crossing swords about *Cool Killers*. Ossie's genius-cat analogy was yet another putdown of Ron Althing's writing.

They had finished eating and were now lounging in front of Nehushta's tiny, black-and-white television set, drinking beer, and intermittently dipping into Ossie's favourite film, the original *All Quiet on The Western Front* which they had happened upon on one of the free channels on the cable system that had been installed by a previous tenant.

Nehushta's place was a one-bedroom flat. The living room – which was actually her bedroom – was Ossie's room during his stay with her. She now slept in the room architecturally designated as the bedroom but which she had converted into a studio when she moved in. When she wasn't building sets for theatre shows, she spent most of her time pursuing the passion of her life, painting, to which she had been a latecomer. Her first degree, from a university up north, was in History. Then she had decided that what she really wanted to do was work in the theatre. So, she applied for a place at St Martin's in London. Since she had no strong desire to act or direct, she had enrolled for the stage design course. Although she thoroughly enjoyed her time at the college, and never once doubted that she was doing the right thing, she discovered during her last term on the course that what she ultimately wanted to do was paint. She liked the mind-boggling challenges that her theatre work often threw her way, designing and building complex sets on unbelievably small budgets and having to meet impossible deadlines. It gave her a sense of being relevant to something that was for her, and every one else involved, more a labour of love than a way of making a living (which was not to say that it would not help if the pay were better). She enjoyed it but she knew that when the time was right, and she would know it when it was, she would say goodbye to the theatre and devote herself to painting.

As she sat with her father in her living room, listening to his impassioned and inevitably opinionated riffs about art, literature and her mother (about whom they talked a lot), she felt comfortable merely sitting there, listening, occasionally interjecting, staring at the telly with the volume turned down.

'The real problem with that so-called play,' Ossie was saying, 'is that it has no heart. Art is always questioning, always seeking new questions to ask, always probing, and perhaps always sceptical, always wary of neat answers. And above all, always redeeming by being humane. *Cool Killers* doesn't even begin to do any of that. Ron what's-his-name thinks being cynical is interchangeable with being sceptical. It isn't. I don't doubt that he's got talent. But talent isn't enough. He needs a dose of humility to his craft, and a pinch of heart, of love, of care for the characters he creates.'

Nehushta looked away for a moment from the scenes of World War carnage unravelling on the screen.

'We lived together once,' she told her father.

Ossie, slightly thrown by this piece of unsolicited

information could only respond with a quiet, 'Did you?'

'We were at drama school together,' she said. 'Ron trained to be an actor, then changed his mind and decided to be a playwright. We started seeing each other during our last year at college. After graduation, we decided to move in together. We were so poor, so utterly destitute, we couldn't afford anything. Then we found an empty flat on a council estate not far from here and we moved into it.'

'You mean the council offered to house you?'

'No. We smashed the lock and moved in.'

'You mean you were squatters?' Ossie looked shocked.

Nehushta nodded.

'How long ago was this?'

'Five, six years ago. I'll show you something.' She got up and went into her studio. When she came back moments later, she had a typescript in her hand.

'What's that?'

'It's a screenplay we wrote — well, *he* wrote it — but it was based on a typical, well, not so typical, night in our lives during that period. You can read it while I nip down to the Mezzanine for some milk,' she said, reaching for her car keys. 'The cab driver's a made-up character. Most everything else is true and did happen that one night to Ron and me.'

She bent over and gave him a peck on the cheek.

She paused by the door. 'Do you need anything from the Mezzanine?'

'No, thanks,' Ossie said.

'I shan't be long.'

She stepped out into the communal hallway, gently shutting the door after her.

Ossie leaned forward and switched off the TV set. He took a deep breath, picked up the screenplay, searched for his reading glasses in his coat pocket and sat back to read the script. It was entitled *One Night*, typed on cheap, frangible, slightly discoloured photo-copying paper.

It was a fairly entertaining though unexceptional writing exercise, overflowing with non-sequiturs and peopled with the not-so-weird and the nearly-but-not-quite wonderful. At least one of the characters was perhaps redundant: a mini-cab driver whose *raison d'être*, aside from driving the Nehushta character (called Naomi) on a clandestine journey to the West End and back, was to tell rebarbative jokes and pointless schlock-horror tales of a monkeyshine, quasi-preternatural slant.

If Ossie had read it as a work of fiction, his sternest observation would have been that Ron Althing's ego had written a cheque that his talent couldn't cash. But he did not read it as fiction. Nehushta had advised him not to read it as fiction. This was why, when he came to the end of the story, his hands started trembling uncontrollably.

5

Although he'd never smoked before, his lips craved desperately for a cigarette.

THE HEIST

1

She knew that something was the matter as soon as she stepped in and the smell of cigarette smoke hit her nostrils. He was pacing about the living room with a pouting, feverish intensity, his back hunched over as if he were suddenly twenty years older; his head lowered, and staring, eyes seemingly shut, straight at his feet. He did not respond when she announced that she was back from the Mezzanine. She went into the kitchen and put the milk and orange juice in the fridge. Then she lit a cigarette and went back to the living room.

'What's the problem, Dad?'

He had stopped pacing around and his gaze was now fixed with disdain on the screenplay, which was still on the floor where he had flung it when he finished reading it earlier. He picked it up and waved it in the air.

'Did you really carry out the things described here?' he asked.

'Yes, Dad,' she replied, having decided to tell him the truth and nothing but.

'You, my daughter, went to a theatre and robbed

people at gunpoint?' His voice rose with disbelief and shock as he articulated each word.

'It was a toy gun, Dad. Nobody was ever hurt and we never intended to hurt any one.'

'He made you do it, didn't he? He talked you into committing this low, contemptible act—'

'You may not believe this, Dad, but it was *my* idea. I talked Ron into it.'

'But why? Why did you do it?'

She shrugged. 'We were broke, and it seemed jolly good fun at the time.'

'Jolly good fun. Jesus! How many times did you carry out these raids?'

'Twice times.'

'I'm very disappointed, Nehushta. Very disappointed. Supposing you'd been caught? Did it occur to you that you could have been caught and jailed?'

'We were caught, Dad.'

'You were? Good lord, what happened?'

'We didn't know that after the first one, most of the theatres immediately installed surveillance cameras in and around them. *One Night* is the account of the second and last one. Unknown to me, I was being recorded, from the moment I stepped into the theatre's foyer to the moment I walked out of the building. It was shown on *Crime Watch*. The neighbours below saw it and phoned the police and within hours we were in a police station being interrogated.'

Ossie fetched two glasses from the kitchen and poured some brandy. He handed her a drink.

'What happened? Did you phone your grandparents?'

'I didn't want to at first, but I didn't want them to hear about it from someone else, so I phoned them.'

'Were they horrified?'

'Were they! Grandma was convinced, like you were, that it was all Ron's fault, that he'd brainwashed me into it all. She and grandpa were very nice about it though, and got me a lawyer. We spent a night in jail and then were released on bail. Within days the story was in every newspaper, and we were being door-stepped by journalists. It was horrendous, a nightmare. As if things weren't bad enough, I discovered that I was pregnant. In court, our lawyers advised us to plead guilty, which we did. Ron's lawyer made a great deal out of the fact that Ron was a gifted playwright who had done what he did out of sheer frustration with the theatre establishment. My lawyer did more or less the same thing with my theatre design background. Largely because I was pregnant, the judge gave me a suspended six-month sentence. Ron got a hundred and eighty hours of community service. The great irony though was that Ron got his first theatre commission and I was asked to design the production as a result of the publicity we got from the case. And we've never looked back since then.'

'And the pregnancy?' he asked.

'Oh,' she said with a shrug. 'I lost it.'

'Oh God, I'm sorry,' he said. They were sitting together on the sofa. He put his arm around her shoulder and hugged her. 'I'm sorry.'

'It was all for the best,' she said in a neutral tone punctuated by a pained silence. 'I wasn't ready to have a baby. I don't know how I would have coped if it had survived. In any case, Ron was quite clear he wasn't ready to be a father. Although when I did lose the baby, when I had the miscarriage, he went into a deep, intense depression. We used to smoke joints regularly. But he took to smoking them all day, then he went into Ecstasy, smack, crack and later on, on prescription, methadone. He became very paranoid. He thought the phone was being tapped. I would come back to the flat and find everything in shreds: cushions, pillows and mattresses slit open, books torn up . . . and he would tell me he'd been looking for bugs. He believed he was being tailed by MI5. We were walking on the high street one day, when he saw a police officer coming up behind us. He started shaking, swearing. He turned round and went up to the policeman. "Why are you following us?" he asked the policeman who looked at him in surprise. "Following you?" he said. "Why would I be following you?" "You tell me," replied Ron. I apologized to the policeman and dragged Ron away. We split up a few days later. I moved back with grandma and grandpa for a few months until I found this flat. I didn't see him for a long time. Not until Hugh, who directed *Cool Killers* mailed me the script and asked me if I would like to work on the production. I read it, liked it but wasn't sure I should take it. I phoned Hugh and asked him if he knew that Ron and I used to live together. He said he did, that he'd sent me the script on Ron's suggestion. Ron himself phoned later that day. He'd straightened himself up, was writing a play for the National Theatre studio, and had been commissioned to write a feature film. And he'd been going steady for a year with this woman, Francoise, whom he'd met while on holidays in France. I accepted the job, and aside from the small matter of him and Hugh falling out big-time, it's been a breeze working on the show.'

'Ron's all right,' she said. 'Okay, just a bit fucked up. But he's good people.'

'I'm sorry I lost my temper,' Ossie said.

'You had every right to be upset, Dad. I would have been upset with you if you hadn't been upset with me after reading *One Night*.'

'Has he shown it to any one?'

'You mean for production? No. But he's threatened to re-write and expand it and see if it doesn't get picked up.'

They were silent for a while.

'Do you think of the baby sometimes?'

'Sometimes. But I got over it ages ago. I have a girlfriend who's had one abortion and two miscarriages. Compared to her . . .' Her voice trailed off into the rash of strange, incontestably red, stars in the whites of his sunken eyes. She reached into her handbag and rummaged through it. She brought out an empty matchbox.

'I've had this for two years,' she said. 'It's got a proverb on it.'

She read out the proverb: '"Yesterday is a cancelled cheque; tomorrow is a promissory note; today is the only cash you have. Spend it wisely." I like that.'

He took the box from her and studied it. 'Excellent advice,' he concurred.

It was well past midnight by now. She yawned loudly and said she was calling it a night. They kissed goodnight and she headed for her room, leaving him to the monstrous munificence of his thoughts.

2

He thought of the slouching shadows of lonesome giants and the radiance of a shared moment, the syncopated silence of selective amnesia and the resonating infinitude of a done deed, the ticking of time and the hypothesis of immortality, the threat of rain and the beauty of a green landscape, the falling out of teeth and the serenity of a toothless smile, the numbing shock of a sudden disappointment and the lingering scream into which an orgasm erupts.

3

He stood up and headed for the bathroom. As he stepped into the tiny cubicle that must have been a design afterthought, a waft of music coming from Nehushta's room rinsed his ears. He had noticed since he came to stay with her that she would often leave her CD player on when she went to sleep. It was too low to impinge on him in the living room, but loud enough to skirt the fringes of his consciousness.

As he peed, he fed his eyes on the images on the bathroom wall: a newspaper photograph of Nina Simone, flyers from various productions she'd worked on, a cryptic cartoon, lost on him, and, his favourite, a watercolour she'd done when she was seven.

Ossie brushed his teeth, rinsed his face and went back to the living room to set up the futon. But it had already been made. She pulled that trick on him every night.

'Thanks,' he shouted. 'I shall retaliate.'

He switched off the light and slid under the blanket. He found, when he tried to sleep, that he was counting sheep.

He worried about the psychologist's appointment that he'd promised to arrange in the morning. He thought about the land of dreams and suddenly he wasn't so sure any more that what he thought had happened had actually happened. Supposing the illusion of the land of dreams had merely been the side effect of some esoteric drug the doctors had administered on him during his coma? He could not bear to think of it. The people he felt he had met during those fifteen years, from Apha, who framed him, to Johni the mass-murderer who did three life sentences and came back the third time as a woman, were as real to him as anybody who had ever been a part of his life. Even if it were proved that they had been mere phantasmagoria, he would mourn them as keenly as he had mourned his father.

He remembered the Nigeria of his youth, a place which was now so far away from him and yet so near. He had not told Nehushta, but the reason he had yet to make up his mind whether to return to his old job was because he wanted to wait until after their African trip. He could not say for sure, but he might decide to move back home, either to Nigeria or to some neighbouring country.

Images from the past kept invading his imagination. He remembered the first time he met Kate nearly forty years ago. He realized with some shock that she was younger when he met her than their daughter was now. He'd met her at a now defunct jazz club in the Grove, Notting Hill Gate. Eric Dolphy was playing in the background and the joint, covered in cigarette smoke and packed with dancing couples, was jumping. Ossie had just realized, after having waited for two hours, that he was being stood up for the second time in a row by his date for the evening. He was sitting by the bar, nursing a beer, his eyes fixed on the door. That was when Kate came in. She was tall (taller in his imagination than she was in the flesh), beautiful in a quiet way, with a milky shock of hair that reached to her shoulders and often fell across her face. It took him all of five minutes to stand up and approach her (long enough to come to the conclusion that she had come to the club looking for someone who was obviously not there). He asked her for a dance. And for another dance. And yet another dance. By the end of the evening he'd left her in no doubt that he was either a pest or someone she wanted to see again. She wanted to see him again.

As Ossie lay in bed reminiscing that night, his memory locked on to that long ago evening and played it back repeatedly.

He thought also about his twin brother Taiye who had died.

Sleep finally came over him, gently swaying him as if he were in a cradle.

4

At exactly three twenty-one a.m. Nehushta suddenly woke up to a deep thirst. She got up, half-asleep, and headed for the fridge in the kitchen. As she went across the living room, which she had to go through to reach the kitchen, she glanced briefly at Ossie and smiled because he looked so at peace.

She tripped over something which, when she opened her eyes wide and was properly awake, turned out to be a thin strip of light that had wandered into the room through the slits in the blinds from the street-lamps outside. She pulled the blinds aside and looked out on to the street. The weather had taken an unseasonably foggy turn.

A strange sense of foreboding came over her. She stood very still.

Holding her breath, 'Dad?'

Moving towards him, 'Dad!'

5

As Ossie Jones crept out of his body and into the mist, his heart murmured till it was silent.

book two

THE WEDDING

1

Mr Meletus had a mental problem. Some time ago, in the now distant past, an obscure bug, resident in the treacherous underbelly of his being, had triggered off a sudden, unannounced and inexplicable rebooting of his psyche. When he emerged on the other side of the feverish delirium into which he had plunged; after sustained institutionalization and a spindling succession of anti-depressive medication, including electro-convulsive therapy in lieu of a prefrontal lobotomy, he was given a council flat in Streatham and visited every fortnight by a care-worker who entertained him with Elvis Presley impersonations. Now officially designated an emotional amputee, Mr Meletus enjoyed psychological crutches in the form of a permanent prescription of non-illicit happiness drugs the supply of which he replenished every other Wednesday, no later than five-thirty in the afternoon, at his local Boots Chemist.

'As I took the down escalator to the Victoria Line at Oxford Circus' – his eyes gleamed as a double-decker bus went past the window of the pub where he was meeting Dada – 'something struck me sharply on the ear. I turned around startled. I saw a pigeon, black, zoom past me, headed – it was clear – for the platform below. I was less than halfway down the escalator when the train pulled into the station. I raced down and jumped into a carriage as the doors were closing. As the train pulled out of the station and into the tunnel, I searched the disappearing platform for signs of the bird. I couldn't see it anywhere. After that, I thought nothing more of it until I got off at my stop. Then I saw a black projectile zoom out of the carriage next door. I ran after it, but it reached the escalators before me and began to head up. Then, without warning, it stopped. It landed and perched on one of those red, circular alarms in the buffer zone between the up and down escalators. I was riding up by now, and I hurried to catch up with the pigeon. As it turned out, I need not have hurried because the bird was waiting, patiently, for me. As I got within arm's length, it rose up like an helicopter, contorted its body into a V-shape, making sure that I saw that this was for my benefit and mine alone, then it made a U-turn and zapped beyond the ticket-barriers, out of the station and on to the street.'

Dada raised his pen from the notebook into which he had transcribed every word Mr Meletus had uttered, and lit a cigarette. 'And?'

Mr Meletus still bore the mental scars of his encounter with the bird. 'It took me all of two seconds to decode the V-sign, and, I tell you this for nothing, I was shocked. Shocked! I turned to the woman standing behind me on the escalator. "Did you see that? That pigeon made a gesture, a rude gesture, at me." She looked right through me and said not a word. Not a word! That's typical, isn't it, of most bloody Londoners! Always in a rat race, always too busy, or too rushed, or simply too self-absorbed to help a fellow in distress. Anyway, I went straight home and told my mother. And,' he leaned forward and stared into Dada's eyes, 'do you know what she said to me?'

Shaking his head, Dada pulled at his cigarette: 'No, Mr Meletus.'

'Mark.'

'No, Mark.'

He leaned back. 'She said that the truth, which neither the woman behind me on the escalator nor I had any way of knowing, was that I was right: the pigeon had indeed made a rude gesture at me. In fact, to be precise, this is what it said to me, it said – in pigeon language, of course – it said, "fuck you" to me.'

He sat up and shook his head as if in doing this he would delete the incident from his memory. 'Can you believe it,' he said quietly. 'A bird said, "fuck you" to me. I mean, what is the world coming to?'

It was Dada's turn to lean forward. But he was only reaching for the ashtray. 'Your mother told you this?'

'Yes.' Mr Meletus, eyes smarting from Dada's cigarette, began to blow the smoke away.

'Is my smoking bothering you?'

'Just a bit.'

'I'm sorry, Mr Meletus.' He stubbed out the cigarette.

'Mark.'

'Mark, how did your mother know what the pigeon said to you?'

'She knows everything,' he said giving Dada a kindly, I-suffer-fools-gladly look.

'Can I talk to her?'

'You could try, but I don't think she'd want to talk to you.'

'Why not, Mr Meletus?'

'Even I only get to talk to her once a week. You see, since she passed away, she's had the most extraordinarily busy calendar.'

'Your mother is dead, Mr Meletus?'

'Mark.'

'Mark.'

'Yes.' He stifled a sob. 'She died five years ago.'

Dada shut his notebook. 'I'm sorry, Mr . . . Mark. It's been . . . illuminating talking to you.'

'When's it going to come out?' He brought out his diary and pen.

'It's too late for the coming issue.'

'I know. That comes out tomorrow.'

'Yes, so look out for it in the one after that.'

'I'm going to buy twenty copies for my friends and family.'

Dada thanked him, on behalf of his editor, for his patronage.

'I'm sorry I have to rush,' he said to Mr Meletus. 'The photographer will be here in half-an-hour.'

They shook hands and Dada headed for the bus stop. He got on the number 35 going towards Clapham Junction. He sat underneath a printed sign that read: 'There will be no change to the frequency of buses,' to which someone had added, in blue ink, 'Or the hassle drivers suffer.'

His next interviewee, who wanted to be interviewed on a bus, had arranged to meet him at a bus stop. This was because the man, an old age pensioner, was to be found constantly travelling on buses. He did this he said, not because he had anywhere to go (and, indeed, he hadn't: his youngest child had recently died aged seventy-two). He was always on a bus for the simple reason that he had a bus pass and wanted to make full use of it.

Dada's editor had asked him to interview the old eccentric.

After that, he was to have a heart-to-heart with a bag lady who had spent over twenty years compiling a list of those *not* to be invited to her funeral. Top of the list was her Cousin Bob – who stole her ice lollipop when she was six. And all Librans, especially her Cousin Bob. And all plumbers, especially her Cousin Bob.

After that, Dada was to speak to a young man who described himself, with disarming honesty, as a 'burglar. And I'm proud of it'. He was taking a year off from prison to finish his O levels. However, these facts, interesting as they were, were not in themselves reason enough for *Care-in-the-Community*, or *Cathy* as it was known, a monthly magazine, to take an interest in him.

The young man's picture was going to grace the pages of the magazine only because he had sent a letter, certified by a psychiatrist to be the work of a genuine psychotic, to the editor. The letter read, in part:

> Spirits not only watched just before a car hit me unconscious and I was injured, a spirit told me in my head not to worry the driver would stop. No charge was taken against the driver. At least 2 or 3 spirits are around me and fly past, 1 or 2 live in my mouth and nose. More bads: they don't let me have friends or get married till death. About 7 years ago, they said 'sacrifice' to me. They control my mouth to insult Jesus 'Bastard' a lot every day, sometimes even shout it out. They are indeed bad & not honest, they admitted they are devils . . .

The letter went on in this vein for several more pages. Dada's editor was delirious with joy when he phoned him about the guy. Dada told him he didn't quite feel like doing this one interview.

'Why not?' boomed his editor.

'He sounds to me like a homicidal psychopath,' Dada said.

'What's wrong with that?' asked his editor, perfectly seriously.

'I don't want to be killed by a homicidal psychopath,' Dada said.

'You should be so lucky, you chain-smoking, booze-swilling, dope-eating, verse-scribbling son-of-a-bitch,' said his editor. 'Do you know the difference between being killed by cancer and being killed by a psychopath?'

'No,' he said.

'The difference is that death-by-psychopath guarantees that you make the front pages of every single newspaper in the country, your friends and relatives appear on the box and, if you're lucky, a film based on your life, starring some young, sexy actor about a million times better looking than you, might even be screened on Home Box Office. Now, you go and die of cancer and see what happens: zero plus zero is what happens. So, do yourself a favour, go do this interview. If the guy does turn out to be a homicidal psychopath but doesn't actually make an attempt on your life, you might even be advised to try and get him to.'

'It's very comforting to know how indispensable I am to the magazine.'

'You're not.'

'You could at least pretend.'

'Why should I?'

Dada needed the money. And desperately too. So, he acceded. When he wasn't trying to write his book (which he often wasn't), Dada was to be found pursuing stories for *Cathy*. The idea for a magazine for 'kooks, nuts, schizoids and Meshuggenahs' came to a former employee of one of the broadsheets after a brief spell as an inmate in a psychiatric hospital. 'When I came out,' he said in an interview on breakfast television, 'I realized that there wasn't a single magazine on the news-stands that catered for people like myself. A magazine that says, "it's all right to be mad, most people are". I felt that there was a paucity of light reading material for those of us who are mentally . . . postnormal. It seemed to me that there was a dire need

out there for a magazine that celebrated the crotchety
in us all.'

And on that premise he remortgaged his mother's
home and founded the magazine. It struggled at first,
but soon enough, after a bumper-size edition that was
dedicated to profiles, in alphabetical order, of the '1000
Most Influential Psychotics In History', its circulation
soared and the ads – mostly from pharmaceutical
companies and psychiatrists – flooded in. The magazine's most popular asset though was its Lonely Hearts
column, through which hypochondriacs sought out
the company of pharmacomaniacs (who have an un-
controllable desire to give or take medicines), mytho-
maniacs found comfort in the arms of pseudomaniacs,
pyromaniacs reached out to hydromaniacs, homicidal
psychopaths (homicidomaniacs) arranged candle-lit
blind-dates at Sushi bars with the chronically suicidal
(autophonomaniacs), and the merely pixillated received
single red roses from the severely demented.

2

Immediately after his interview with the old man who
felt that he would be wasting his bus pass any time he
wasn't using it, Dada headed back to Brixton by tube
for a funeral. Although he was a few minutes early, he
was still the last to arrive. His Aunt Moni, the
Heckler's mother, was there, in the undertaker's intimate chapel seated with various other members of the
extended family, consisting of long term UK residents
(like Aunt Moni, Uncle Tinu and Cousins Tokunbo,

Kilani and Lade), and visitors from Nigeria (like his other aunt, Bola, and her daughter Risi).

And of course there were the Mabogunje, the wealthy end of the family. His uncle, Chief Prince Bode Mabogunje M.Sc. Ph.D. MLL. MQD. OFR (Order of the Federal Republic) had lived in exile now for over ten years. He had been a government minister under the last civilian administration in Nigeria during which time he managed, through sheer prestidigitation with public money, to acquire two houses in Hampstead, a golf course near Inverness, a holiday home in Provence and various businesses of questionable worth in North America. His single most notable achievement during his time as minister was the award of a contract, to a childhood friend, for the construction of a multi-storey office block. Unlike most contracts awarded in those days, this had the virtuous distinction of having been realized and on target as well. It wasn't until the day when Uncle Bode, flanked by police outriders, turned up in his ministerial cavalcade to cut the ribbons and declare the building open, surrounded by dozens of cameras, waited upon by a desperate coterie of scheming and ingratiating hangers-on and a troupe of scantily clad female dancers, fresh bananas sticking like flags out from their busts, who had been bussed in to provide 'cultural activities', that the discovery was made that the twenty-storey edifice, architectural masterpiece though it was, was in need of a lift, of which there was none. The sub-contractor to whom the task of building the lift had been apportioned had simply imploded from the face of the earth, turning into a kite on a string, or the echo of a fart, in some place far from Earth, pausing in Lagos only long enough to collect a substantial down-payment on the contract. When the soldiers came calling at the seat of power soon after, with armoured-tanks only just smaller than their egos, and with murder in their eyes, Uncle Bode was among the first members of the overthrown government to take off his shoes, *Al'hamdulilla*!, and run for his life. For a long while, no one knew where he was or whether he was alive. Then a year later he surfaced in London, Ontario, with his wife Aunt Kemi, who used to be a high class hooker, and whose past was strewn with the wrecks of men whose hearts she'd broken and whose homes she'd ruined, from Kafanchan to Conakry, and Kutiwenji also. She'd been a beauty in her day.

During this time of lying low, Uncle Bode had systematically liquidated all his assets with the exception of a five-bedroom house in Hampstead to which he now relocated with his family. His children, Dada's cousins Sade, Toun and Dapo, had always lived there anyway, having been educated at various English public schools and at Oxford and Cambridge and, in the case of Dapo, who was thicker than a deep-pan pizza (with garlic on mould where his brain should have been), at a phantom but ubiquitous, and suitably expensive, private university that produced knowledge to order and wisdom to the highest bidder, and had a customer-loyalty card, which existed, honest to God, at a discreet address off Bond Street.

Within the family it was rumoured, nudge, nudge,

wink, wink, that Dapo was Uncle Bode's only true biological progeny.

Dada's interaction with the Mabogunje strand of the family was limited to family occasions such as the funeral today. For one thing, they could not fathom why, and it was totally beyond them how, any person of any worth could live in the Wild Southwest. And Dada didn't do much for global understanding or the reputation of Brixtonians when at the last party to which the Mabogunje invited him he'd turned up with three friends who smoked so much pot that when the police came knocking they told them they'd simply followed their nose. And from five streets away.

The Heckler's mother, Aunt Moni (to whom Dada had been sent by his parents from Lagos when he was seven years old), belonged to the less well-off end of the family. She and her husband, Uncle Jonah – who lived up to his name by being swallowed by a great fish off the coast of Badagri during a visit home in the early eighties – had lived in the UK since the fifties.

Dada greeted Aunt Bola, the youngest of the aunts and uncles, and whom he hadn't seen since her last trip to London two years back. She brought the usual greetings from home (and the usual '*and-finallys*' which consisted of long shopping-lists from relatives down on their luck and childhood friends running on empty), and kisses from his siblings and his mother, who was getting old and wanted to know when he would visit and if he was still seeing that girl and wasn't it time they got married and started a family.

Aunt Bola was a university lecturer, which meant

that her monthly salary was no more than thirty or forty pounds. Her trips abroad were possible only because her husband worked with Nigeria Airways, the prophetically named Flying Elephant, which entitled members of his immediate family to generously dis-counted tickets. Aunt Bola's caustic wit, for which she was notorious within the family, wasn't noticeable today. Dada knew it couldn't be because of the funeral. He turned to her daughter, Cousin Risi, who it was usually impossible to shut up once she had opened her mouth. But Risi was all pauciloquence, and so crest-fallen and underwhelmed, he thought she might be ill or suffering from a toothache.

Her mother leaned towards Dada and explained Risi's uncharacteristic mood.

'She's failed her university entrance exams for the third year running,' Aunt Bola confided. 'She applied for a place in Pharmacy at the University of Ife but failed to achieve the minimum required score.' She gave Risi a withering look, which Risi saw off with an insouciant shrug. 'But that's not the amusing part. The amusing part is that when the last results came out, and she found out she'd failed again, she tried to kill herself with an overdose of Paracetamol.'

'What's funny about that, Aunt Bola?' He looked at Risi with an attempt at an expression of sympathy. She responded by rolling her eyes derisively. She'd never liked him, and he'd never much cared for her either.

'Don't you see?' Aunt Bola sighed. 'She fails to secure a place on a pharmacy course, she then bungles a suicide attempt with *pharmaceutical* products because she got the dosage wrong! If she'd had the brains to get the dosage right, she would at least have had the honour of going to her grave having proved that we were all wrong, she wasn't a complete idiot and, yes, she did have an aptitude for pharmacy, or a brain, after all.'

A judicious cough by Aunt Moni signalled that all muttering should cease.

The officiating priest entered the chapel. He was from Aunt Moni's church, a Pentecostal denomination called the Angelic Church of Christ, where they spoke in tongues and were taken by the Spirit.

He walked barefooted and was dressed in a soutane, a long white cassock with golden tassels that trailed after him like a bridal train. His Bible was embroidered with flowery little crosses cavorting around the tetragrammaton, the secret, ineffable names of God.

The pallbearers, carrying the casket, glided in on silent feet.

And the Heckler's funeral began.

3

The funeral procession continued from the undertakers' to the cemetery. Aunt Moni, together with Prophet Moses, the officiating priest, and Aunt Bola and her daughter Risi, went in the hearse. Uncle Tinu and Cousins Tokunbo, Kilani and Lade followed in their car. And Dada had no choice but to travel in the Mabogunje's car. Toun, the oldest, a dentist, was driving. Sade, the only girl, who worked in the City, sat in front with him. Dada was sandwiched in the back seat with Uncle Bode and Dapo, whose only visible source of income was his father.

Aunt Kemi was home in bed with a cold ('Mark my word,' Aunt Bola had whispered to Dada earlier, smiling sweetly at Uncle Bode, 'that's not all she's in bed with.')

Uncle Bode and Dapo now resumed a conversation whose genesis Dada had not been privy to.

'The particular fixation I take to the present situation in Nigeria,' Uncle Bode was saying, 'is that we have a wild monster claiming to be the head of state. It's an unpardonable insult. I can never allude to him as head of state. It makes my blood jump each time I ruminate about it. It is not just because he is a soldier, be that as it may, nor because he's perpetrating yet once again the archaic hegemonic interests of the feudalist phenomenon, it is just the very fact that here is someone who has been part and parcel as it were of the most corrupt regime the country has ever been calamitized with, now succeeding in this whole musical chairs of Chinese whispers where the left hand doesn't know what the right hand is doing.'

To which Dapo, who seemed to know what Uncle Bode was talking about, responded (raining spittle on Dada, in the process): 'But, Dad, y'get me though? Y'know y'have t'get actively involved in the oppositional struggle, so t'speak, you 'ave to be in close proximity, in a manner a sayin' . . . Y' 'ave t'muck in . . . Y' 'ave t'get pro-active, y'know wha' am saying?

Y'can't joost sit there and stand. Y' 'ave to put your line on the head . . . y'know wha' am sayin'? You can't have your cake and swallow it, y'dig wha' am sayin', Dad? Y'get me though?'

The two Mabogunje in front were squirming in their seats.

Uncle Bode now turned to Dada. 'So, young man, what is your considered opinion on the matter?'

'What matter, Uncle?' he asked.

'This vile kakistocracy that now has the socio-political-economic life of Nigeria as a puppet on its apron rings.'

Dada frowned thoughtfully, trying to figure out the least dangerous way to extricate himself. Finally, he decided, fuck it, and said: 'I haven't got the faintest notion what you're on about, Uncle.' He waited for Uncle Bode to order the car to stop so he could throw him out. Instead, he burst out laughing.

'You see?' – patting him on the shoulder and turning to Dapo – 'His head is so full of mareejjoe-Wanna smoke there is no more space, or for that matter, room in his mendulla oblongata for ponderance or rumination.' He added, in a wondrous tone, 'Like father, like son!'

Dada turned to him. 'I didn't know my dad smoked.'

Uncle Bode doubled over. 'He didn't. He just wasn't inclined towards excessive susurration.'

Translated from Uncle Bode-speak this meant that Dada's father had not been given to much talk.

'Wasn't he, Uncle?'

'No. That's why he could not emulate me and go into politics. Consequentially, when he kicked the bucket, it was as a pauper, with no ways and means, nor any money to his name that he went knocking on heaven's door. Being the Good Samaritanian person that I am, I generously paid for his burial ceremonies out of my own pocket.'

Sade, who was, according to family legend, the product of an act of indiscretion between Dada's father and Aunt Kemi at a New Year's Eve family do, now turned to Uncle Bode. 'Leave the poor man alone, Dad. And keep his father out of it.'

A dangerous glint came briefly to his eyes. He was not nearly as stupid as he liked to come across. His buffoon act was a mask, from behind which he had ensnared the world as he plundered his way to wealth. He belonged after all – in the words of Aunt Bola – to an Exclusive Club of Thieves who stole an entire nation and sucked its future into a vacuum cleaner called the International Monetary Fund.

Dada looked out the window. The car had stopped.

They had arrived at the cemetery.

4

The coffin, stained a faint mahogany, was made of pinewood. It had brass fittings and golden handles. A felt-mattress, handmade and fit for a king, was spread inside. The coffin was ready to be lowered, bumping from one scraggly side of the wall to the other, and backward and forwards, into the dug earth.

A photograph of the Heckler smiled at them from the hand-quilted silk shell-shaped pillow where his head, were he in the coffin, would have rested.

Prophet Moses walked in a circle around the coffin, swinging from a chain a dome-shaped incense burner that filled the air, and their noses and lungs with the pleasant but dizzying and overbearing scent of sandalwood, eucalyptus, frangipani, coconut, lemon grass, patchouli, cinnamon, mango and myrrh. He muttered a rapid and inaudible swelter of words, which Dada knew, having been dragged by Aunt Moni to church when he was a kid, as a form of glossolalia, the gift of tongues.

Aunt Moni was weeping quietly; stricken it seemed, with pure, unutterable grief.

The rest of them, who were there only because it was a family matter, and family were there to be there, stood in a huddle behind her, stilled not so much by the ongoing ceremony as by the place they were in.

She commenced on a busy, moving speech about the Abiodun she used to know, the Abiodun who was born at St Mary's hospital in Paddington, one gloriously stormy morning twenty-eight years ago, when the wind roared and strummed all night, celebrating, she was sure, the arrival of this child she'd tried but failed three times in the past to bring into the world. He was a few weeks premature, and the doctors and nurses had feared that things could go wrong again. But her Faith was in the Lord, and the Lord spake unto her, and the Lord sayeth to her, cry not my daughter, wipe thy tears away . . .

As Aunt Moni continued to talk, Dada looked around him, at the faces surrounding him. It all looked, he thought, like a wedding.

He looked at Risi, who had tried but failed to end it all with an overdose of Paracetamol. Her mother, Aunt Bola, was to find out, a week later, when they had returned to Lagos, that the reason her daughter had been so pensive during their trip to England was not, as she thought, because Risi was still dwelling on the bungled suicide, but because she was pregnant and wasn't quite sure who the father was.

He looked at Uncle Tinu and Cousins Tokunbo, Kilani and Lade, distant family, so distant, there were no whispers, rumours or legends passed down about their fathers, or their mothers' fathers.

Standing beside them were the Mabogunje: Uncle Bode, who would suffer a massive heart attack in five years, undergo a quadruple bypass, make an astonishing recovery and be sufficiently strong to go back to Nigeria, now under a new dispensation, to a hero's welcome from the same people whose very future he and his friends had mortgaged in perpetuity to the IMF.

He looked at Toun, the dentist, who would give it all up in four years time, denouncing his father, and leaving his wife and children to join a Hare Krishna Ashram. His wife would hate him, and forgive him. His children would hate him till the end of their days. His name would turn to vapour in the family's memory.

This, plus a longing for home, would precipitate Uncle Bode's heart attack.

He looked at Dapo, who was destined to live to be ninety-two, never having done a day's honest work in all that time. He would die happy, in his sleep, with a smile on his oily, fleshy face, having remembered as he drifted into eternity a joke that he would hear today (in three hours time, on the drive back to Hampstead).

He looked at Sade and she smiled at him, cryptically, when she caught his gaze. In seven years time, she would come to Dada's funeral, after he'd been stabbed by a gang of muggers (median age thirteen) who thought, but were wrong, that he'd dissed them under his breath. The murder weapon would be a twelve-inch, blackcoat-anodized knife with honed finger-grips and a Combo-Edge-serrated blade described by aficionados as 'bad to the bone'. At Dada's funeral, Sade would hold hands with his widow Lola, whose orbit of existence and Dada's would only intersect during the last two years of his life, five years after he flew up one night, and sailed to the moon.

Sade would say to Lola: 'He was my half-brother, but he never knew it.'

He looked up and saw that Aunt Moni had finished her panegyric and that Prophet Moses was now speaking. As his ears regained their bearings, he realized that the prophet was reciting a traditional Yoruba elegy, which he'd heard before, at the funeral of Uncle Jonah, the one eaten by a great fish.

'The hunter dies,' Prophet Moses was saying, 'and leaves his poverty to his gun. The blacksmith dies and leaves his poverty to his anvil. The farmer dies and leaves his poverty to his hoe. The bird dies and leaves its poverty to its nest. You have died, Abiodun, and left us abandoned in the dark. Where are you now? Are you the goat eating grass round the house? Are you the motionless lizard on the hot mud wall? If we tell you not to eat earthworms it's like asking you to go hungry. But whatever they may eat in heaven — partake with them. A dead body cannot receive double punishment: if there is not cloth to cover it, there will always be earth to cover it.'

As Prophet Moses came to the end of the dirge, Aunt Moni's voice crackled, like a bird's wings as it leaves the ground, and soared into a hymn:

> No Grave Can Hold My Body Down!
> No Grave Can Hold My Body Down!
> When the Trumpet shall sound
> And the dead in Christ shall rise,
> No Grave! (No Grave!) No Grave!
> No Grave Can Hold My Body Down!

And they all joined in except for Risi, who seemed inconsolable. She was lost in the moonless wilderness of her thoughts, seeking not a way out but the firefly of mercy.

5

The day after the Heckler's funeral Dada sought him out at the swarming caravanserai of megaphone-wielding pundits by the tube station. The last time he'd seen him the Heckler had bags around his eyes,

and was effortlessly worsted by the militant lactovege-
tarian activist he had chosen to tackle. 'Well, well,' he
said later to Dada: 'I never thought the day would
come when I'd be forced to have scrambled egos for
breakfast. And by a vegetarian, too.'

'You need to sleep more, eat more and drink less,'
Dada told him.

'I've always said no to the Just Say No brigade, but
coming from a degenerate like you, I guess I'd better
listen up,' he said.

His target today was a group of elegantly suited
apostles of the Nation of Islam in dark glasses.

'Truth is no respecter of persons,' the leader, surrounded by his lieutenants, was saying, 'and whether
you like the truth or not, it is—'

'I like the truth, that's why I read the Sunday
papers.' A lie, by the Heckler. He stopped reading the
papers when Dada stopped buying them.

' – important that we find ourselves on the side of
truth—'

'Go ahead, black man,' interjected one of the
lieutenants staring stonily at a woman blowing kisses
at him.

' – and we don't allow ourselves to be caught out
on the side of a lie.'

'Who is "we"?' asked the Heckler.

'We are members of the Nation of Islam,' said the
leader. 'And the Nation of Islam is a body of people
who are determined to tell the truth even though the
world is averse to the truth.'

'Go ahead, brother.'

'We are a people who despite the reputation of this spot in Brixton—'

'Precisely what reputation and which bit of this spot do you have in mind?' asked the Heckler.

The leader, who was beginning to take strong exception to the Heckler's existence on this planet, kept his temper but lost his syntax. 'Is for people to come here and speak nonsense,' he roared at the Heckler. 'Is for people to come here and sow confusion among the masses of the people.'

'You *what*?' the Heckler shouted, knowing he had scored an accidental hit and trying not to look too pleased with himself.

'That's right, brother,' concurred a lieutenant scowling at the Heckler.

'Is for people to come here and speak tripe!'

'Tripe?'

'Is for people to come here and make mockery of God—'

'No, you're mistaken, I've just come here to take notes.'

' – make mockery of righteousness, make mockery of principles. However, in the Nation of Islam, we have no intention of walking that particular road. We say if that's the road you want to walk then you will walk it without us. And we invite you to go along and you will find many speakers here today, many mockers, many fools—'

'There's one over there but unlike you he's not wearing Ray Bans.'

' – that you can gladly go and be foolish with. That

you can go and listen to. But if you wanna hear us, then you will hear a word which is powerful and full of truth. And you might be able to grow and develop—'

'Go ahead, brother, go ahead!'

'—but if you want to continue that foolishness which is in the world today, then you are invited to go elsewhere. They will come from far and wide' — fixing the Heckler with a hex — 'just like that little nasty voice you heard a few seconds ago.'

'Go ahead, brother.'

'And the idea is to try to sow confusion, the idea is to try to deviate us from our destination and our path.'

'Go ahead, brother.'

'In the Holy Quran, the Devil promises Allah . . . he says that I will come at them, from their left side, and their right side and behind them—'

'Randy old bugger!'

'—and I will cause them to deviate!'

'Deviate, brother, that's right, brother.'

'And Allah says, whoever will deviate with you, I will fill Hell with all of you. And so today, we in the Nation of Islam, we refuse to be deviated by the Devil.'

'Go ahead.'

'You're not deviated *by*—' screamed the Heckler, but was shouted down by the leader.

'And the Devil can shout and scream as much as he likes—'

'Go ahead, black man.'

'But we know him today.'

'That's right.'

'And we refuse to be deviated by the Devil . . . who has no power.'

'Teach, black man, teach.'

'I have a book in my hand called the Holy Quran.'

'Go ahead, black man, speak on that.'

'It is a book full of wisdom.'

'That's right.'

'It's also full of racism, misogyny—' shouted the Heckler.

'Shut up!' said one of the lieutenants.

'It is a book that was revealed one thousand four hundred years ago, to a divine prophet of God—'

The Heckler's voice rose again. 'It says in that book, go into your wife—'

'The Prophet Mohammed—' The leader was screaming now.

'Go ahead, keep teachin'!'

' – had received a revelation—'

'Keep teachin'!'

'Keep goin'!'

'And he revealed to us a good Word.'

'Go ahead, black man, teach.'

'And that word is to be found in the Holy Quran.'

'Go ahead, black man.'

'And so we are gonna give you a Word today, from this Book.'

'That's right.'

'We are gonna give you a word today from another book—'

'That's right.'

' – A book called *The Theology of Time*—'

'That's right.'

' – by the Most Honourable Elijah Mohammed. And' – holding the books up – 'this book verifies this book. This book backs up this book.'

'Go ahead, brother.'

A member of the crowd, a Scouse, raised his hand. 'Why do you oppress people who are of different opinion than yours if you say that you're preaching to everybody?'

'Those of you who have something to say, who would like to question us, when we have finished what we have to say, we will allow a question and answer period—'

But the Heckler was having none of it. 'Why does it say . . . white faces will belong to the believers and black faces will belong to the unbelievers? Tell us that. It appears twice in the Quran.'

The leader paused and spoke slowly and directly to him. 'We will invite your question when we have finished what we have to say.'

'Keep teachin'!'

'Those of you who are here to lecture us, well, we are not here to listen to a lecture, we are here to give a lecture—'

'Go ahead. That's right.'

'That's why we're standing on the platform.'

'It's not a very informed one is it?'

'If you desire to give a lecture we suggest to you that you get your own platform and those who want to listen to your lecture I'm sure will come and listen to you.'

'Mmmm.' The lieutenants, nodding. 'Tell him, brother, tell him.'

'But we are not here to be lectured—'

'You are here to propound the very racism you claim to be fighting,' came a shout across Dada's shoulder by a man behind the woman behind him.

' – and so if you know you have a preponderance of words that you wish to express you are really speaking to the wind, because we will not be listening to what you have to say. We will be saying what we have to say. And we will remind those listening that it is very simple to understand that when there is a pack of dogs, and you take a brick and throw it among the dogs, only the dog that gets hit yelps.'

'That's right.'

'And so if you hear constant barking from behind you or in front of you—'

'I used to be a real dog but I'm all right nooooow!' growled the Heckler, like a route of wolves.

' – that is a dog that is getting hit by a brick today. And listen to the dog, for he is in pain.'

The Liverpudlian raised his hand again. 'I just don't understand why you need this protection around you.'

'Well, let me explain that too. The gentleman said – I call him a gentleman, I hope he is one—'

'He didn't say, he asked.'

'He said, why do we need all of this protection around us? It is a very good question and one that deserves an answer.'

'So let's get on with it.'

'As you know, Almighty God, Allah, in his beneficence and mercy—'

'Gave you all travelcards.'

'—builds into his creatures the device and the
mechanism and the wherewithal for self-defence. Self-
preservation is the first law of nature.'

'Fine,' said the Heckler, 'but nobody here is defend-
ing themselves except you.'

'The Nation of Islam is a controversial body of
people. We have many enemies—'

'Including Malcolm X?'

'—who have made themselves manifest. And we
have the hidden enemy.'

'That's right, brother, that's right.'

'And there are some of our enemies here today.'

'That's right.'

'Most of them are Australian tourists,' said the
Heckler, smirking.

'They would like to see the end of us. And so, like
any intelligent persons, we exercise the right of self
defence.'

'That's right.'

'But nobody wants to fight you.'

'And we protect that which we love. And any
intelligent human being protects that which they love.
In the houses in which you live you have a security
device on the window. Some of you have alarm
systems—'

'Some have big dogs,' said the Heckler, trying but
unable to resist the temptation to bark.

'These brothers here are here to protect the word of

God, and a speaker of God, because as a black people—'

'Go ahead, black man.'

'Throughout our history, and our sojourn here in the Western hemisphere, whenever a leader came up among us, whenever a leader came to speak on our behalf, those who did not like black people moved against that leader, and that leader was subsequently lied upon, vilified, ostracized, isolated and then assassinated.'

'Speak, brother, speak!'

'This is the history of black people in the Western hemisphere. The Honourable Marcus Garvey lived here and was destroyed because they did not want black people to have good leadership. Martin Luther King, who taught to love everybody, had his brains blown out because there wasn't adequate protection put around him. Malcolm X, who taught black people a knowledge of themselves, was ultimately assassinated by the United States government, who sanctioned and paid—'

'That is not true!' Several voices followed and with flowery expletives.

' – lackeys,' looking pointedly at the Heckler, 'from the black community to carry out their dirty work. And so today we are learning from the lessons of history, we are determined that when you killed Malcolm X, when you killed Patrice Lumumba—'

'Go ahead!'

' – when you killed Samora Machel, when you killed Kwame Nkrumah, when you killed all our great leaders, we say never again!'

'That's right, brother, go ahead.'

'And so today we have defence and protection around those of us who will speak on behalf of the masses of our people.'

'That's right,' said the Liverpool man, 'but the brave men in front of you can't stop a bullet.'

'And so! That is the reason why we have these brothers here today. And whether we can stop a bullet or not – if you don't believe we can stop a bullet then fire one!'

'I won't do that, I won't do that because it's not—' The Liverpudlian, looking rather at a loss.

'We ain't playing today!' shouted the leader. 'And it's not for us to stop your bullet, we have a God on our side! And our God can stop any bullets . . . in fact you haven't got a gun big enough!'

'Yes, sir!'

'Because the scripture says who God is for, no man can be against.'

'Then you don't need the protection,' ventured the Liverpudlian.

Which seemed to incense the leader even more. 'Whatever you do we are intelligent.'

'Go ahead, brother.'

'We intend to make a righteous noise in Brixton today!'

'Tell them, brother.'

'Tell them!'

'And if they come with their noise, we will make a better noise!'

'Teach them, brother.'

'And they will be drowned out because today is the day of truth!'

'Teach, brother, teach!'

And then someone piped: 'Where are your Caucasian brothers?'

'We're here!' responded an old tramp, gingerly scratching a life-size pustule on his nose, which had been broken and reset, badly, so many times it was beginning to assume the shape of a bend in a river.

The crowd laughed and applauded and the old tramp raised his hat and took a bow.

'Why are there no women with you?' cried a woman, standing beside the Heckler.

'The lady asked the question why are there no women with us at the moment.' Obviously exasperated, the leader considered the question. 'The simple answer to that question, Madam, is that ... contrary to popular belief, our women do not walk ten paces behind us. Our women are not covered up like tents. Our women are not ill-treated. We love our women. We are taught that no nation can rise higher than its women. The nation is not judged by the condition of the man, the nation is judged by the condition of the female. Because the woman is the one who produces the nation, without the woman there would be no nation—'

'My question,' said the woman, with an Irish accent, 'was, when you gonna 'ave a woman speaker on yer platform?'

'Good question, Madam, good question. All women are sacred. And that's why the Earth is called Mother

Earth, that's why the universe, the stars, are *she*. Because it's the universe that gives birth to all the planets. And so women are held in high esteem. Our women are so greatly loved and elevated they sit on a pedestal. And that's why you don't see them. It's not because they are put down, it's because they sit on a pedestal and—' Now turning on the Heckler out of whose mouth a quip was about to unleash: 'Shut up or leave.'

'Is it something I said?' the Heckler wanted to know.

'I think he just doesn't like your locks,' Dada volunteered. And, speaking of which, his dreads did look in dire need of tough love.

'Wanna buy me a drink, *hombre*?' said the Heckler, turning to Dada.

'What you need, brov, is some dog food.'

He went down on his knees and started barking at Dada.

'Stop that, Snoop,' Dada said.

Dada brought out a leash and slipped it round its neck.

The dog followed him, wagging its tail.

6

Half an hour later they were sitting at a table at Eco café in Market Row, talking about the funeral while making short shrift of two huge pizzas.

'So I was buried yesterday.' The Heckler, practically swallowing an entire slice without so much as a chew, was quite intrigued. 'Did she phone or did she mail you the invite?'

Aunt Moni had phoned Dada only the night before the funeral. He was in his flat, on the floor, naked, relaxed and supine; smoking a joint and settling down to watch an eighties film called *Flirt*. Since he possessed neither a TV set nor a VCR, this consisted of shutting his eyes and skimming through a drop-down catalogue of scenes, a transfinite list of set pieces, from an odd variety of films tabulated and stored between his left ear and his right, equipoise, between unreliable recollections and the limpid inventions of his imagination. He was sifting through these reels, projecting them onto the wall of his mind, the wide-screen across which they would unfold, when the phone rang.

'Yes?' Freeze-framing the adolescent Thandie Newton and Nicole Kidman, he snapped into the phone.

It was: 'Aunt Moni! How you de?' he said to her in pidgin, to which she had an aversion.

'Your father, may he rest in peace, did not send you to England to come and speak like a common ruffian, like a scoundrel from the gutter,' she used to say to him in the days when he lived with her, before the Heckler and he became (in her words) 'prodigal children'.

'Dada, how's your work?' Her voice, as always when she spoke to him, or to him about her son, was filled with a quiet sorrow and scoured by the desiccated rinds of every dream that (in her perception) she'd seen them kill, every hole she'd seen them dig that she'd tried but failed to stop them from falling into.

He began to tell her about the *Cathy* interviews that were lined up for him the following day.

But she cut him short. 'You know that I wasn't asking about that, Dada. I was asking about the book you've been writing since the day you graduated from university. It's almost eight years now, Dada, you're not growing any younger. Is it nearly finished?'

Knowing that she knew that he was lying, he said: 'Yes, Auntie, it is nearly finished.'

'Every morning when I wake up and every night when I kneel in prayer, I ask the Lord of Hosts, Almighty God, I ask Him, "Where did I go wrong when I was bringing up my children?" You, Dada, and your cousin were such sweet children when you were small. What happened? When did it all begin to go wrong? When your uncle, may God keep his soul, and I came here in the fifties, we came with nothing but our dreams and were determined to make something of our selves. We studied by day and worked at night. We worked hard and studied hard. Lord knows we worked hard. From our meagre earnings, we were able to send Abiodun' – the Heckler – 'when he was born, to the best schools this country could offer. And when the doctors told me I could no longer have children, and your parents agreed to send you to live with us, we worked even harder, sometimes keeping four jobs between the two of us, so that both of you could have a good education. We wanted to give you both the best start in life. Was it all in vain, Dada?'

'I promise you, Auntie, I am happy with what I'm doing. I swear, Auntie.' Which was more or less true.

'But what happened to your dream to become a doctor?' she asked. 'Why did Abiodun leave his job to become a bum on the streets?'

'We were kids, Auntie. Now we are men. Our dreams have grown.'

'What about *our* dreams, Dada?'

'I'm sorry, Auntie. All I can say is that I will finish the book. I will try and make you proud of me someday.'

'I'm glad to hear you say that, and I *am* proud of you, Dada. At least you still have it in you to talk about dreams. But what about your cousin? Why did he give up on everything?'

Dada hesitated. This was dangerous territory. He knew why the Heckler had 'given up on everything' but he wasn't about to go into that with his aunt.

He decided to say nothing. Which was when she dropped a fragmentation bomb into parts of his being that he didn't even know existed.

'We are burying Abiodun tomorrow,' she announced.

'You're *what*? But I saw him only—' A deep howl, hurtling from his throat, burst out, and was immediately pulled back in a choking grip that threw him into a coughing-spasm that stung his eyes into a flood of tears.

'Abiodun is not dead,' he heard Aunt Moni say. He emerged, shaken, relieved and mightily pissed off, from the *fata Morgana* into which he'd been dipped.

'Goddamn it, Auntie, if he's not dead, what the fuck did you mean you were burying him?'

He had never sworn at her before. The shock, when she regained her voice, was cached in her breathing.

'What's come over you, Dada? Why are you all so angry with me?'

'I'm sorry, Auntie, you gave me a shock, that's all. I'm not angry with you. Forgive me. Please.'

'Prophet Moses' – of her church, the Angelic Church of Christ – 'had a vision. The Lord spoke to me through him.'

Dada said: 'And what did the Lord have to say?'

And immediately bit his tongue.

She ignored the sarcasm. 'The Lord told him to tell me that the only way to bring back the old Abiodun is to bury the impostor that is inhabiting his soul now.'

He asked her how the Lord proposed that they carried this out.

'By holding a symbolic burial and a funeral,' she said. 'I have managed to buy a plot at a cemetery, and I have spoken to an undertaker.'

The undertaker was apparently a member of the Angelic Church.

'Then what happens, Auntie?'

'That is not for us to say, Dada. The Lord has asked us to be patient. The Lord's ways are intricate and mysterious.'

'Have you told him?'

'Abiodun?'

'Yes.'

'I have.'

'And?'

'You know your cousin.'

Dada turned now, at Eco's, to the Heckler:

'What was your reaction when she told you?'

They'd finished eating. The Heckler was lighting a cigarette.

'Amusement?' Like it was a question. 'I was mildly amused. She actually wanted me to be present. Can you beat that? She wanted me to be present at my own funeral. I said, mother, mother . . . And she left me alone. So, brov' – he offered Dada his pack – 'how did my funeral go?'

'Well.' Dada lit a cigarette. 'It went well. I even read a poem.'

'You read a poem?'

'Yes.'

'One that you wrote yourself?'

'Correct.' Blowing smoke in the Heckler's face.

'Fuck me! When did you write it?'

'Yesterday?'

'Have you got it on you? Feel like sharing it with us?'

'If you insist.'

'I do?'

'All right then. Just this once though,' Dada said. 'It's called "Journey".'

'I'm with you, pal. Take me on that trip.'

'"Journey",' Dada said.

'I want my ashes scattered
Far and wide in a stream, or the sea, or in a sunny clime,
Or just here and there; with Monk, Miles, Mingus or
      Trane, or the Duke,

Or Lady Day or nothing but the sound of silence bidding
    me
Farewell and welcome on this journey,
In this loop, through these hesitant steps
That lead me back the way I came.

'Like it?' he asked the Heckler.

'Not bad. Not bad at all. Personally though, I'd have preferred some sort of pop music – the trashier the better – not yet invented, blasting to a bass line of heckles.'

'A bass line of heckles?'

'That too hasn't been invented. I'm glad you found your muse again, did it tell you where it'd been?'

'Time to 'fess up. I lied, I wrote that five years ago.'

'Asshole.'

'And I didn't read it yesterday. But I wanted to.'

'Well, as Anon – a.k.a. *they* – said, it's the thought that counts. You wanker.'

'You haven't heard everything,' Dada told him. 'Remember that dream I told you about?'

'You're Mr Fucking Dreamer, you are. Which one of them dreams are you asking me to unforget?'

'Remember the one where I'm in Bah Humbug having a bit of a fall out with Midé? And then this beautiful woman, this *vision* walks in with her dad?'

'Vaguely. If I remember rightly, that was over a year ago. And Midé says it wasn't a dream.'

'Fuck, Midé. Yep, that's the one. Well,' he said, 'guess what happened at the cemetery yesterday?'

'You're not gonna tell me you ran into her ghost, are you?'

'I did better than that. I ran into her.'

'You know what you need? It's therapy, is what it's called.'

'I'm serious, H. I swear!'

'You know what am gonna do you for, coz?'

'What are you going to do for me?'

'I'm going to sit here and listen to you talk about this imaginary woman that you're in love with.'

'Thank you.'

'Then am gonna go out on the town with it. I'm gonna dine out on it. How about that?'

'Shut up, listen up.'

7

They ordered coffee.

BOOK THREE

THE SMOKE

1

'Your funeral,' Dada told the Heckler, 'was over in less than an hour.' Afterwards, he continued, Aunt Moni invited them all over to her house for snacks. But the thought of spending another minute more with Uncle Bode and Dapo was simply too much for Dada. He pleaded a previous engagement, an assignment for *Cathy*, and promised to catch up with them later, if he finished early.

He stood outside the cemetery gates and waited until the Mabogunje, whose stretch limo was at the rear of the small procession, had driven off.

Then he headed for the bus stop.

He must have been in deep thought trying, and no doubt failing, to exorcise the demon of Uncle Bode and the day's unrelenting catalogue of bizarrerie from his memory. Or merely agonizing over the three stories that he had to do for *Cathy* because he needed some change in his pocket (not to mention the bills, the bills!), which, furthermore, had to be on his editor's desk before the ('foocking') weekend ('or you're foocking fired!'). Whatever it was, he had walked past her, and gone on walking for quite some time before the extraordinary image interpolated by his eyes into the blue expanse of his mind had swung him round in a sudden start. And there she was when he turned round, smiling at him, the woman he had met in his dream.

'Are you who I think you are?' she asked.

What? he thought, crackling his knuckles (the message he'd transmitted to his brain was that he would like to wipe his nose).

She reached into her shoulder bag and pulled out a recent issue of *Cathy*. She flipped through it quickly, hurriedly, stopping on a page which had, at the top of a relatively sane interview he had done with a man who was convinced he wasn't himself (but the restless soul of a Tamagochi tortured to death by a ten-year-old apprentice psychopath), a grainy, not particularly flattering, black-and-white photograph of Dada.

'That's you, right?'

'I . . . yes,' he said.

'I'm Nehushta,' she said, shaking his hand.

'You read that?' the last word said with an italicized inflection. His heart was rising and sinking at the same time. His breathing which was loud and slow and then fast and frantic had quietened into a serial discontinuity of half-beats.

'I don't just read it,' she said. 'I'm a subscriber. I swear by it.'

'Well,' he said, lost for words.

'What are you doing here?' she asked, returning the magazine to her bag.

He began to explain. 'We, my family . . . had a funeral . . . sort of.'

He was mumbling so much that the only word she could make out was 'funeral'.

'Oh, I'm sorry,' she said. 'Was it someone close?'

'Was *who* what?' he asked.

She put his strange behaviour down to the shock of bereavement. 'The funeral you were attending,' she said. 'The person that died.' She was reaching out to place a condoling hand on his shoulder.

'No one died.'

Her hand pulled back. 'No one died?' She reached into her bag again and rummaged through it until, announced by a rattle, her car keys materialized like a magician's rabbit in the cup of her hands. 'Do you need a lift? That's my banger' – pointing – 'I'm heading towards Brixton.'

She went to fetch the car, and a minute later pulled over and pushed the door open. He got in beside her.

'Are you all right now?'

His mind and his lips had by now renewed all bilateral ties. 'I'm sorry,' he said, 'but I've been trying to explain the inexplicable. What I was trying to say, is that the funeral I was attending was a purely symbolic one.'

She reached for a pack of cigarettes in the glove compartment. 'Smoke?' Her hand touched his as she gave him the pack. 'Could you light one for me as well, please?'

He lit the cigarettes.

'Thanks,' she said. 'A symbolic funeral? What's that?'

'It's a long, crazy and complicated story, and,

believe me, you don't want to hear it. Anyway, enough about me. What were you doing back there?'

She didn't inhale so much as suck in the cigarette. 'I was visiting my parents' graves, well, more my dad's really 'cos it was the first anniversary today, but since they are buried right next to each other, till death do us join sort o' thing, I did a look-see on mum as well.' Each word tripping out fast on the heels of the last, as if fleeing from a house on fire, with no perceivable pauses between thoughts or sentences, no rhythm to the rhyme.

'Mum died, oh, years ago, of cancer and Dad of a brain haemorrhage which if we extrapolate from Hempel's Paradox that a purple crow is a confirming instance of the hypothesis that all crows are black means I think and you best know that I'm congenitally immune to Meningitis Poliomyelitis Cirrhosis Alzheimer's Anaemia Creutzfeldt-Jakob Disease pleuro-Pneumonia Parkinson's Heart Diseases Yellow Fever Leukaemia Tuberculosis Repetitive Strain Disorders Restless Legs Syndrome Stiff Man Syndrome and, yes, you guessed it, the common flu.'

Seeing, through the corner of her eye, that Dada's jaws and eyes (one dropping, the other widening), were in the process of distending his face into a Bali mask of catalepsy, she punched the steering wheel and burst out laughing, which, when he saw that, threw him into a shaking and crying fit of laughter that left him gasping to the floor.

She slowed until he'd regained his breath.

'Sorry,' she said. 'It's a trick I play when I'm trying

to break the ice—' pause, quietly, '— and also to say that I don't want to talk about my parents.'

She had certainly broken the ice. 'What do you do?' he asked, still trying to stifle the spasms from his lungs.

'I paint,' she told him. 'That's how I got interested in your magazine—'

'I don't really work for them, I mean I do' – he felt the need to explain – 'but not full-time. I like to think of myself as, above anything else, a failed poet.'

Glancing sideways at him. 'And how do you define a failed poet?'

He shrugged. 'I don't know. I've been trying now for, oh, since – if the years were money, I'd be a millionaire – give or take a few months, to write a book, a collection, something tangible, something I can hold in my hands and say, I wrote that, I must be a fucking poet.'

'And?'

'So many years down the sewer and not even a damn punctuation mark beyond the first letter of the title.'

'Which is?'

'Changes by the day. I've tried everything between A and Z.'

'Do you get depressed about it?'

'I don't get depressed about things like that.'

'What depresses you?'

'Waking up at three in the a.m. and finding that I've run out of cigarettes, *that* makes me positively suicidal.'

'I was under the impression that your magazine was written by—'

'The insane for the deranged, yes, but it's also required by law to be an Equal Opportunities Employer.'

' – you mean they hired you *because* you're black?'

'Fuck they did. No, they hired me because they thought I could write the sort of stuff they wanted, and because they needed to hire at least one person who'd never been sectioned under the Mental Health Act, I think it's called. I qualified, but only just. During my last year at school, the head teacher sent me to see the school shrink. I went, not knowing why I was being sent. The shrink, when I got to his office, looked at the file he'd been sent about me, and said, "What is this obsession you have for the IRA?" I told him, truthfully, that I didn't know who or what the IRA was. "The Irish Republican Army," he explained testily. "Surely you know who they are. It says here that you've been going around addressing your schoolmates with a raised thumb salute and the shout: IRA." "Oh," I cried, "you mean *Irie*! But, sir, that's just a patois form of greeting." "Well," he said, twitching his moustache, "well." '

Dada laughed at the memory. 'Anyway, tell me, what's painting got to do with *Cathy*?'

'Have you got a minute?' she asked.

2

Her flat was packed, which is to say bursting, with paintings and sketches and the tools of painting. It was clean but untidy, higgledy-piggledy but not bereft of charm.

He recognized many Brixton landmarks on the canvases: The Brix (which used to be St Matthew's church, built in 1824 to commemorate — legend had it — the battle of Waterloo), the Ritzy Cinema (which came into existence as the Electric Pavilion in 1911), Electric Avenue, the first shopping street to be lit by electric power. And the Academy, a concert hall which started life in the twenties as the Astoria Cinema. And several scenes from the rambunctious Market Row and Granville Arcade.

Most of the paintings though were portraits of people, many of whom Dada knew either as the Brixton Undead or in the course of his job for *Cathy*. Here were characters like Prinze 'The' Big Mac, who was as crazy as they came, and used to hang around the station all day and half the night with a big, fatuous grin on his face, saying to passers-by, 'Admit it: you think I'm crazy, don't you? Don't you? I know you do.' And the blandsome and affable Mr Pepler, well dressed and quite respectable looking, and never to be found without a copy of the *Financial Times* tucked underneath his arm. Looking flustered and in shock he would accost you with a carefully rehearsed tale about his pocket having been picked and, terribly sorry, old chap, but you couldn't possibly lend him a pound for the bus home, could you?

And countless others.

'As you've probably guessed, I first encountered many of them through your column,' Nehushta said, as they came to the end of the small, guided tour.

'Did you get them to sit for you?' he asked.

'Some of them, yes. Most of them though, I simply stalked for days with my sketch-book.'

'But what's the point of it all? Why the loonies?'

'I started it all shortly after Dad's death. I was just fascinated by, I suppose, fragility and resilience. I like to think of it as a celebration of Brixton through its used, abused and contused.'

'I call them the Undead.'

'Maybe they are. Would you like something to drink? I've got beer, rum and brandy. Or . . .' She paused briefly in omphaloskepsis, or the contemplation of one's navel as an aid to meditation. Then, having contemplated, and on a whim deciding, what-the-hell, to trust him, she continued, 'Or you can have a burn, if you're partial to skunk.'

'Oh no, I'm on the wagon—' he began to say, then: 'Did you just say skunk?'

They were in the living room. She went out through a back door that led into a sprawling conurbation of wild flowers, exotic plants and thin, dwarfish etiolated trees of indeterminate origin and indefinable redolence.

She came back inside with a terracotta bowl which, when she took the lid off, turned out to be sanctuary to several kilos of fresh, pungent and eminently smoke-able marijuana.

He whistled. 'Bloody hell, all that for you alone?'

She pulled out, from her shoulder bag on the sofa, a pack of king-size Rizla (which for some reason unfathomable had the legend 'No. 1 in Africa' printed on its top right-hand corner).

'Up until a year ago, I was a stage designer.' She was sitting, in lotus position, on the parquet floor, constructing the joint. 'Then Dad died and I decided after that to do what I'd always wanted to do: quit theatre and paint full-time. With the money he left me, I could afford to do so. Barely a month after I quit, I began to get all these calls from actors, directors ... thespian friends who, when I worked with them, would occasionally ask me to do them a favour and get them a quarter, or an eighth of smoke from my dealer. And that, apart from to find out how I was doing, was what every single one of the calls was about. Turned out customs had intercepted a big consignment coming in from the continent, and there was a massive, huge drought on the streets. I was quite pissed off at first, 'cos I'm thinking, "Fuck, do they take me for, a drug dealer?" Then I check my Filofax and realize that I know dozens and dozens of people, from the several shows I've worked on, who are *active* burners. And so I said to myself, why not support my work—'

'I.e. painting.'

'I.e. painting, by dealing on the side? To this group of relatively decent, generally copacetic folk who, after all, just wanted to have a good burn at the end of the day.'

She had finished rolling the joint. 'Do the honours?' She passed it to him.

He did. He took a draw, and went: 'Wow-wow-woww, this is . . . wowww. Where's it from?'

He passed it back to her and she took a toke.

'What do you know about weed?' she asked.

'I smoke 'em, get high.'

'There are basically two types of weed,' she said, 'indicas and sativas. The difference between an indica and a sativa is THC, Tetrahydrocannabinol, or Delta 9 as it's also known. It's the thing that gives you a high, like the alcohol in wine. It's the reason cannabis is illegal. On its own, THC gives you a very clear uplifting high. It's a CBN – a cannabinol, but there are other kinds of CBN, which, if they're added to THC in small amounts, slow down the rate the THC gets into your head. What this means is that you get a more sedative relaxing high. Indicas have high THC and a fair bit of CBN as well. So, what happens when you smoke them is you go into a heavy, sleepy high. Your eyes go red and you just sit there, feeling completely relaxed. That's what gives with indicas. Then you've got the sativas that don't have any CBN. Or very little. The THC rushes into your brain and you get this very cerebral feeling, it gives you a more powerful, space-y high, rather than a sedative high. Sativas grow along the equator. Or in tropical zones. The African variety, one of the top two strongest sativas in the world, is from the Congo Basin, Malawi or Nigeria, strong sativas. Very powerful. They go straight into your head, and you're on a very *trippy* high. Beautiful weed. And then there's the Southeast Asian sativa: Thai, Colombian. Everyone loves a Thai, it's got a unique high of its own. Makes you laugh a lot. A grown-up person just starts acting like an idiot. Great stuff. And with them, the THC content is about ten, eleven per cent. That's the strongest natural THC you're likely to get. Now, in Holland and America, over the years, people have managed to mess around with natural THCs, through inbreeding projects, and produce skunks. Now, you can't grow sativas indoors. The bastards'll grow to about ten to sixteen feet tall. Yeah? You've got to have fields of it. Unlike indicas, which produce short, five-foot plants, with very dense flowers, sativas produce next to no flowers. You get more off an indica; it's smaller, and it only takes half the time to mature. So people wanted to grow it indoors. But they didn't want pure indicas. Sativas are better. So what they did was they did a breeding project where they crossed cannabis indica with cannabis sativa to create plants, a few plants, and then inbred them. So, they managed to produce a plant like . . . like the Afghani. An Afghani is your classic indica. Short, high-yielding, dense flowers, beautiful smell. Beautiful, skunky smell. Pungent. But: with a sativa high. So, through inbreeding, they managed to get a plant with a great sativa high that's short, stocky and manages to produce high THC. Higher than you would get in nature, like sixteen, seventeen per cent. That's skunks. Powerhouses, they are. There're several varieties of skunk: skunk number one (to infinity), Big Buds, Northern Lights . . . Skunks are weeds that have been produced rather than grown naturally. They're wicked. And hard to get. So, the two types of weed are indicas and sativas. A lot of London gets indicas, you know: black, resin, rocky, that kind of stuff. I personally don't like that stuff. A lot of the high is just feeling sleepy, it's not actually being high. I prefer sativas. Or skunks, which is what you're smoking right now. What do you think?'

All he could come up with was a hoarse: 'Wow-wow-woww.' Then, just so she wouldn't think he couldn't hold his smoke, he plundered far off corners of his mind for a random selection of words that might assume meaning and attain coherence when articulated. 'How do you get hold of it?'

There, smirked his brain, that wasn't so difficult, was it?

'There's a neat, simple pecking order to the game.' She was rolling another joint. 'In London and the Home Counties, there are five big boys each of whom moves a tonne a week. That's a thousand kilogrammes times five. Which they then sell to the next guys down, who'd be looking to buy a hundred keys each at maybe a grand a key.'

'So the one tonne guys end up making, what, a million pounds?'

'Give or take. Then these hundred-kilo guys will sell *their* hundred kilos to five-kilo people. At about fifteen hundred a key. So, they're making a hundred fifty grand on their hundred kilo. And then the five kilo people sell quarter kilos to street dealers. For about six hundred a quarter, so they're getting about twenty-four hundred back. Me, I'm strictly five kilo. Weekly sales, added up, about eighteen hundred pounds.'

'Profit?'

'Depends. The bigger the quantity a client buys the less money you make on it. On the average though, it comes to about seven hundred pounds a week.'

'That ain't half bad.'

'I am a very small, very low-key dealer. I don't go near any of the heavy stuff, like coke, crack, heroin or smack. I don't take too much risk, I sell to decent people and' – getting up – 'I'm a pretty nice gal, really. And a nice gal ought to be able to support her work. Speaking of which' – she glanced at her watch – 'I've got to get back to work.'

'Just when I was beginning to get comfortable.' They'd been together for over three hours. 'I guess I'd better be going.'

'Do you want a ride to the tube?' she asked.

'No, thanks. I can walk. I live not very far from here.'

'You live in Brixton?'

'Always have done.'

'Strange we haven't run into each other until today.'

'Yeah.' He was tempted to tell her about his dream but decided not to.

'I'm curious though,' he said, at the door. 'Why did you tell me all this stuff when you hardly knew me and all that you knew about me was that I'm a journalist?'

She smiled.

'Because I've got you sussed,' she said. 'I know where you're at.'

With a painfully straight face: 'Really?'

'Yes, Dada. I know the question you're going to ask me, if not now, the next time we meet.'

'We are going to meet again then?'

'Not unless you don't want to. I was going to ask you if it would be all right for me to go with you to your next *Cathy* interview, if there's one coming up.'

'There should be a couple next week, and you're welcome to come along, I'm sure they won't mind. So,' he was beginning to sweat on the nose again, 'what was this question I was going to ask you?'

She laughed. 'You sure you want me to—'

'Go ahead. I'm going to deny it anyway.'

'Okay. Let me think.' She didn't have to. 'You were going to ask me if I was seeing someone.'

Fair cop. 'Are you?'

'Yes.' Laugh. 'Sorry.'

'Hey,' he said smiling, 'I didn't say you were right. I didn't say I was going to ask you any question.'

'No?'

'No. But since you brought it up, is it serious, this someone you're seeing?'

She nodded slowly, several times, smiling.

'There. That's settled then. Now I can't wait to get home and get hold of that brandy.'

They exchanged phone numbers.

'*Arrivederci*,' she said in Italian.

'*Ate a vista*,' he responded in the only Spanish he knew. 'Thanks for the smoke and a brilliant evening.'

He stepped out the door and headed home, somewhat groggily, under the bluish twilight sky that, he decided, existed in the mind of the universe, or in the imaginations of nine million Londoners and the Weather Channel.

3

After seeing Dada to the door, Nehushta flopped on the sofa in exhaustion. It'd been a long day. She had been up since just before dawn so as to catch Mr Bill, a peripatetic idiot savant who was to be found every weekday during the morning rush hour standing outside the tube station, touching commuters for money by enacting one or more of his several specialities, which included reciting and offering the meanings, origins, synonyms, antonyms and, where applicable, usage and abusage of every single word under the letter H in the Oxford English Dictionary. He would even throw in the homonyms, his ulcers permitting. But that was in winter. In the summer he sold words for a living. He would take his usual spot outside the station, beside the newsagent's stall, and standing there he would whisper words into the ears of passers-by in exchange for a modest honorarium, the average being ten pence per word (though some had been known to buy whole sentences).

One man bought a paragraph. It was a birthday gift for his wife. Others simply came back for more words.

One woman bought three words then came back the following day to ask for a refund. Courteous as ever Mr Bill said, 'Very well, madam, may I have my words back?' The woman stamped her foot in fury: she'd forgotten the first word, she couldn't pronounce the second, and the third had escaped through her nose when she sneezed from a bad cold. Mr Bill took pity on her and gave her three new words for free. One had been damaged in transit and suffered from a fractured syllable so he replaced it with a new word. The woman was speechless with gratitude. Later that day, in the quiet of his bunk under Waterloo Bridge he repaired the broken word with a needle and thread. It was the best he could do. The needle pierced his finger and he watched the blood drip but did nothing to stem its flow.

He would usually disappear from Brixton immediately after the rush hour. He'd been spotted twice on Oxford Street going through rubbish bins for stray, homeless or discarded words. A Chinese tourist, who took the Polaroid evidence back to Peking to show her friends, captured him once on camera in Covent Garden performing an illusion with words. He coughed out the words, which took the shape of his cigarette-stained teeth turned into birds bereft of wing. He stammered the bloodied words into the palm of his hand, polished them into clearness with a stainless handkerchief, and gifted them with wings, and sent them flying into the great void beyond sound or silence, where all words uttered in the universe, and in all languages on the planet, are stored for all time, or forgotten for ever.

He was seen once in Ladbroke Grove haggling with a second-hand words seller over the wholesale price of a mouthful of words. He got them cheap; they'd been damaged by rain. He laid them out in the sun to dry. One of the words had a broken wrist, which had healed into a fist unable to open. Mr Bill nursed it back to health: it shook hands and opened doors and warmed itself before a fire and waved at friends going away.

Another time, he stood outside Buckingham Palace and tried to flog an entire chapter to a member of the Royal Guards. The guard appeared not to hear him. Mr Bill did not know that the guard was hard of hearing and that he was speaking into the guard's deaf ear. Mr Bill went home a failed salesman. A deep melancholy came over him that night and he sat up in bed unable to sleep. He comforted himself by composing new thoughts with old words. He slept after that and woke up in the morning with a smile on his face.

4

Nehushta was not quite sure why she had embarked on committing to canvas the faces of this band of nameless vagrants that drifted like flotsam on the sporadically turbulent streets of Brixton. It began, like many decisions she had taken since the night her father died, on a caprice. The idea had come to her during her trip across Europe (on which a small urn containing her father's ashes accompanied her). The idea came one night in Amsterdam, while she was having a hot bath in her hotel room, a cheap, seedy but well-kept joint in the Leidseplein.

Her decision to quit the theatre and have a go at painting had happened almost immediately after Ossie's funeral when his solicitor had invited her to his office and read out the will (which, eerily enough, her father had signed only the day before he died). As she travelled through France, Italy, Germany, Switzerland, Austria, Spain and a succession of Scandinavian land-scapes, she had been aware of a certain unease, a restlessness that was taking possession of her. She identified its cause, which was a desire for specificity, the need for a game-plan, only when, as she sat in the bath chortling to herself about this and that and the other, its cure occurred to her: why not spend the next year or so, when she got back home, trying to capture the recurring faces on the streets around her?

She would do this over a year or two, or until it ceased to interest her. She had no plans for an exhi-bition. She reckoned she could afford to live on her inheritance for about five years if she was careful, which she usually was with money. She could always go back to theatre, or do something different with her life, if painting turned out to be a mistake after all. Her capricious decision to subsidize her art by dealing did not necessarily buy her more time; it simply raised the stakes. It meant that not only did she have to fraternize with the certified unhinged, she was inviting felons into her back garden, and therefore the law into her front room.

After spending a couple of hours by the tube

station drawing sketches of Mr Bill she went back to her flat, changed, and then headed for the cemetery. It was a year since Ossie died, and she hadn't visited in a while. She spent the day there, sitting on a mat, by his grave and her mum's, finishing *To the Lighthouse*, which she had started reading aeons before but had never managed to find the time to finish. It was a pleasant sunny day, much like the day when she came with Ossie to visit her mum. She had conversations with both of them, but only from within her.

It wasn't purely by accident that she had run into Dada outside the cemetery.

She had spotted him as she headed for her car. She had seen him wave to the cortège as they drove off. She had seen the look of relief on his face when the last car disappeared.

When she saw him go towards the bus stop (she recognized him from the photograph in *Cathy*) looking mildly distracted and preoccupied, that was when she decided – again on a whim, out of no motive she was consciously aware of – to stop and talk to him.

But it wasn't the first time she'd run into him in the flesh. That happened over a year earlier, on the day she and Ossie had visited Kate together. After the visit, when they got back to Brixton, and after Ossie had endured a haircut, which he said would leave permanent scars on his ego, they'd gone to Bah Humbug for coffee. It was late afternoon, just before it usually got busy with the dinner crowds.

She did not notice Dada immediately. She vaguely remembered seeing two men, black, having what appeared to be a heated discussion at a table to the far-left corner of a shadow to the middle of the peripheral vision of her right eye. She remembered ordering a cappuccino for her dad and an espresso for herself (or was it the other way round?). Then, at some point during an engrossing conversation with Ossie, she heard raised voices.

She looked up.

It was a waiter saying, in obvious bemusement and irritation, 'You're joking, aren't you?' to one of the two black men she'd noticed earlier. One of them was no longer there. The one remaining who, when she looked at him now, appeared quite drunk, shook his head at the waiter who seemed to be getting angrier by the second.

'Listen, mate,' she heard the waiter say, 'if you want her name and number, why don't you go and ask her yourself?'

'Brilliant suggestion,' said the sozzled man getting to his feet. 'I shall do just that.'

She had no idea what the altercation was about.

It wasn't until months later, when she stumbled across *Cathy* while browsing through the magazines at her local newsagent's and was introduced to his column (which she happened to like) that she found out Dada's name.

5

On that day in Bah Humbug, however, she watched uninterestedly as he got up from his table. Then, as he began to stagger towards the bar where she and her father were seated, it began to dawn on her that the oenomaniac might actually be entertaining thoughts of approaching her. It wouldn't have bothered her if she were alone. She would simply have upped and left. But she was with her father who was in full paralinguistic flow on a snapshot moment from her childhood.

The waiter had seen the look of alarm in her eyes and was now moving to catch up with Dada and stop him. In the event, he needn't have bothered and she need not have worried.

As Dada reached the last table between him and the bar, he crashed into it, and was flung back across the room by a convergence of acute inebriation, ill-luck, a metal table whose cannibalized ancestry included self-projecting missiles, plus various marginal and unknown quantities (such as the lightness of his soul, the simplicity of his terror and the exceptionally strong tail wind). He was knocked out cold.

6

Nehushta finished her coffee and, cutting her father in mid-flow said to him, 'Drink up, Dad. Let's go.'

The Visitant

1

'You ask me I'd say she sounds pretty wild, is all I can say,' said the Heckler.

They had long left Eco's, and had been to Red Records to browse idly through the latest hiphop licks. They'd also stopped by at the bank next door attempting through the hole-in-the-wall to tease out some funds from Dada's tacitly agreed but unauthorized overdraft. However, instead of spitting out the reassuringly crisp lapis lazuli (of the paper variety, made from cotton fibre and linen rag) that Dada requested, the automated teller-machine fixed him with a crafty grin and advised him to get in touch with the issuer of his card.

Dada, who knew no shame but may have passed through it on his way to righteous indignation, slipped his cash-point card back into his wallet.

'Fuckers know my pay cheque's due in on Monday.'

'You're lucky it didn't eat your plastic.'

'It wouldn't dare do that.'

'I believe you.'

'You may snigger all you want. Do you know how much money they make off me?'

'Much?'

'Much.'

'And plus interest?'

'And *plus* interest. Plus they be thinking, how do we know he's not going to win the jackpot tomorrow?'

'You're not.'

'How do you know that?'

'You don't play the lottery.'

'No. But they don't know that. Do you?'

'Play the lottery? You know I don't.'

'Well, you know what they say: it *could be* YOU.'

'Yes, just like The Plague: why me?'

'Still not told Auntie?'

'Nonono – nope.'

2

An open-top Ford Fiesta, equipped with a stereo system and speakers in its boot twice the price of the car (multiplied by the square root of the cost of the driver's gold-fillings), went past them blasting a chant by KRS-One:

> I'm not number one.
> (I'm sorry, I lied)
> I'm number 1, 2, 3, 4 and 5 . . .

Upon which these avowed cynics, being the hardened optimists that they were, and mistaking coincidence and noise-pollution for a talisman from God, extemporized one more number to make up the required six and immediately dashed into Hussain Newsagent's ('In God We Trust, Everybody Else Pays Cash') to register those magical numbers on the national lottery. They did not win, but might have done if they'd played 6, 7, 8, 9 and 11 instead. And the number 12 or the bonus 10.

They bought cigarettes. Dada, who was paying with the last coins he had on him, found that he was one penny short.

'Don't look at me, Chancellor,' said the Heckler. 'You know my giro ain't due till the millennium.'

'Don't leave the country,' cracked Hussain JR, whose name was Mahmoud, deferring settlement of the outstanding amount till an indefinite next time.

They crossed the road at the traffic lights between McDonald's and Pizza Hut.

'Think you stand a chance with this babe?'

'I don't know.'

'I fear for you, Che.'

'Why?'

'I see dodgy karma, M. Mao.'

'Why?'

'I see your arse being whupped, Citizen D.'

'Shut up, H.'

'Call me Cassandra.'

3

They saw, across the road, Midé beckoning to them. He was standing in front of his bookstore whose motto, 'Fighting Ignorance since 1477 (it's taken longer than we thought)', was printed underneath its name, which announced itself simply as 'Books'.

'Should we pretend not to see him?' suggested the Heckler.

'You know, Midé, he's going to come running after us.'

'If he starts on one of his stupid stand-up routines, I swear I'm a respond with a squib of hydrogen, nitrogen, oxygen, methane and carbon dioxide flavoured with a mystery cocktail of pungent spices.'

'You fart near me, H, I'm liable to kill you.'

'Trust me, Von D, it'll be a breath of fresh wind.'

Midé was now calling out to them: 'I heard the news. I'm sorry.'

'What news?' asked the Heckler.

'About your cousin,' he said, facing Dada and ignoring the Heckler, 'it's a great loss, naturally. We didn't always see eye-to-eye but I had a lot of respect for him. He was a good man, a kind man. He once said to me when I was in trouble – and I'll always remember this – he said, "Midé, if there's anything I can do, you know where to find me. There's nothing I wouldn't do for you—"' Now he looked at the Heckler. 'He kept his word: he did nothing for me.'

Then, rolling into a belly laugh, Midé continued, 'Don't take this personal, guys, but someone has to say it: your family is seriously fucked UP!'

Midé dashed back in the store, where he proceeded to make an announcement. 'Ladies and gentlemen, behold,' he said, pointing with a flourish at the Heckler, 'the resurrection man! Most of us can but dream of it, Jesus Christ – as my mum so fondly calls the Lord – took three days to do it, but this man, ladies and gentlemen, this man died and was buried only yesterday. And here he is with us, barely twenty-four hours later, in the flesh, resurrected, fresh and ready, New and Improved, to save the world all over again! A round of applause and a loud *Amen* to the Cryonic Christ of Brixton!'

'Did I just say fuck you?' asked the Heckler as Midé pushed him forward to take the applause, which he did, and after which he went about the store, trekking across valleys of knowledge tucked in between mountains of dross, and liberally dispensed blessings to the blighted of spirit and absolution to the heavy of heart. He even found time to cure a legion of lepers.

But, since most of Midé's customers didn't know who the heck the Heckler was, and weren't in the least bit interested to find out, the Cryonic Christ soon threw Midé in a major panic as Midé watched potential sales evaporate when the customers started fleeing from the cloying beneficence of the Christ of Brixton to Book Mongers nearby, which was run by a bearded Irish–Bostonian who treated books like guide-dogs, and dogs like a man's best friend, and friends like the kings of the earth.

'What shall I do?' Midé asked Dada as Christ restored sight to a blind woman who had been browsing through a James Baldwin first edition when the miracle occurred, and who promptly absquatulated to the coffee bar next door as soon as she could see.

'See? See!' shouted Midé. 'He's driving my customers away!'

The Cryonic Christ of Brixton commenced on his Sermon on the Mount, making do with a trellis chair in the absence of hills or rocks.

4

Out on the street, a busker went by, pushing a synthesizer in a baby buggy.

THE SPEECH

1

The week after he met Nehushta, Dada sat down in his flat one evening, chain-smoking and staring at his computer screen and at a mini-recorder from which the lyrical cadences of a somnolent voice slurred a farrago of smooth increrudition, into his ears.

Dada had been dispatched earlier that day to interview a man his editor had somewhat cryptically described as a 'dervish for our times. He's a tad low on serotonin, though.'

In an earlier life the man's name was Delroy, but now he went by the name of Ras Joseph. His dreadlocks reached down to his knees, falling lazily down his back in an animated cluster of dark, furious question marks.

And this, from an edited transcription, was what he had to say.

'Long time I been hearing about de half dat never been told, ya'understan? It start by dese two people dat I met. Dey tell me 'bout de Virgin Mary, otherwise known as Elizabeth de Cathalic, a queen dat once was crowned in dis country who dey murder while she on de t'rone. But because she is the Blessed Virgin Mary,

Jesus Christ sorta reincarnate her back from de dead.
So she a back 'ere now.'

'So Mary is still here?' Dada lit a cigarette.

'Yeah,' said Ras Joseph. 'She's still here but it's like
at de moment, her own people lookin' for her to
destroy her again. Murder her again – ya'understan?
So, she's sorta been disguising herself. Going around
de place, different type of body and more like de Black
Madonna. She have de power now to change herself to
a black woman or a white woman – ya'understan me?
It's like if she fear dey are gonna discover her when she
white, then she woulda change to black, ya'understan?
Dat's why you get new, live Black Madonna. But it
still Mary, who actually play dat same part, y'know
what I mean. After dey kill 'er off, she couldn't live
with dese people any more so she have to go to Africa
to live with her son down dere, you know w' I mean.'

'Her son?'

'Selassie I.'

'When did this happen?'

'Books dey can tell you 'bout maybe when dey kill
Elizabeth de Cathalic. You can hear about how long
Mary she actually were crowned and queen. And why
dey did kill her and tings like dat, ya kna I mean. But
it never tell you dat she was the Blessed Virgin Mary.
Ya kna I mean. All dey call her was, Mary Elizabeth
de Cathalic. Ya kna I mean. But now I met dis woman
who would tell me her life story. Ya kna I mean. It
sorta lift sense away from nonsense. Ya kna I mean.
Because dere is a book who also say dere was a queen
down here by name Mary Elizabeth de Cathalic, true,

which dey actually killed fe true, ya kna I mean. Anyway when I was sorta lookin' back to everyting, everyting sorta give me a little bit of understandin' about the Blessed Virgin Mary. Fe true, really dey murder her. No doubt about it, dis woman I have met who came down here Mary Elizabeth de Cathalic, she a ghost all right, ya kna I mean. Dat's it. She is here. No joke about it. Ya kna I mean. Now she have dis man wid her, right. He's like' – turning now to Nehushta, who was bent forward, etching into her sketchbook – 'your colour, ya kna I mean. He's brown man like, who she have as her son. Jesus Christ. Who reveal himself to me as Selassie I, ya kna I mean. So dat actually makes sense again, ya kna I mean. Dis match up wid what Rastaman been preachin'. And a Rastaman, Jesus Christ, who actually reveal himself as Selassie I, ya kna I mean. I coulda never understand why Rastaman been saying Jesus Christ was Selassie I. Ya understand. But when I met dis woman, de white woman, and dis man wid 'er, de brown man, den I could see sense outta nonsense. Yeah, Jesus Christ could be a brown man and not a white man as dese white people teach me from when I was a kid goin' a school. So sense outta nonsense. It seem like Jesus Christ was a brown baby, coming from Africa, fe true, ya kna I mean. So dis message really is to de whole entire earth because what Jesus Christ really want, is if we can get dese people make it back, the Blessed Virgin Mary way. Also the Blessed Virgin Mary would like it dat de people dem mek it back 'er way, ya kna I mean. 'Cos, dat is de way of God, ya kna I mean.

Jesus Christ is a black man really, ya kna I mean. And him mek himself born from Mary. A white woman baby which is like a black man baby, and a white woman baby. Mek de baby was a brown baby, ya understand, which dey would call half-caste. But Jesus Christ wanting to call him brown. 'Cos he himself did mek himself, no one did mek him, ya kna I mean. Dat's his name – Mr Brown Man – ya understand? Like, dere was a song he say:

> Walk through the classroom
> Whole and sweet
> Who so English
> Sweetie Charlie Brown!'

2

Dada, sweating from the sheer mental exertion required to decipher Ras Joseph's samizdat, lit another cigarette, tugged at the mouse and reached for the keyboard into which, after having muttered to himself the words, 'Oh, fuck it, I'm just gonna have some fun,' he tapped the words:

'Sensational New Claims: The Virgin Mary Was Murdered . . .'

Now wholly seduced by the god of mischief, he proceeded to compose a long, tangled and deadpan exercitation, a compendium of Black counternarratives and conspiracy theories beginning with the more incendiary of Ras Joseph's mellifluous detonations and morphing in free-fall into a litany of Grand Plots by

The Man against People of Colour, including but certainly not confined to the invention of the HIV virus in a nameless laboratory on the farthest edges of the Nevada desert, somewhere east or north or perhaps to the south of Truth and Good Intentions, and on the flip side of the Bill of Rights (which is, in any case, Void Where Prohibited By Law).

3

When the article came out in an 'Ethnic Special Edition' of *Cathy* called *Mad fe Real!*, which was published to coincide with the Notting Hill Carnival, the shit – and Dada's job – hit the fan. The magazine's phone lines were jammed for days with calls from incensed readers, many of whom also took the opportunity, thank you, to cancel their subscriptions. Two dailies and a Sunday broadsheet, antipathetic to one another, tacitly resolved to bury the hatchet in the head of a common enemy, and intervened with editorials about political correctness gone too far. The *Noise* newspaper, the Monumental Minaret of Black Blandiloquence (which we hate to love), consolidated its irrefragable claim to being Britain's best black weekly by reprinting on its front-page excerpts from the piece, under the title: It's All True, Jesus Christ Was Black! A prominent right-wing cultural critic denounced it on TV as 'risible, reactionary twaddle'. The *Yo!* Press, an enterprising outfit specializing in eminently forgettable pop fiction by black writers, issued it as a clothbound audio book with pictures.

Dada received a phone call from his editor who had been on vacation in Ibiza when the piece was published. The call began and ended with the poignant and alliterative 'Phew! Foockin' fired,' the first word being onomatopoeic for 'you're' when uttered in phury.

4

A famous black comedian turned it into a sketch in which he played Jesus. The Imam of Bradford reprimanded him for ridiculing a prophet.

THE DATE

1

Dada, freezing but putting a brave face on it, was standing outside Brixton tube station, waiting for Nehushta. He wasn't sure if he was early or if she was late, but he'd gone through three roll-ups, his newly embraced carcinogenic of choice, since he arrived at their rendezvous. His mood wasn't quite as sunless as the weather, but it was getting pretty dusky. The clouds, which appeared to have descended just above his head, did little to lift his spirits.

There were no signs of the preachers and mystics, or the *Big Issue* vendors ('Bigger than the biggest, better than the best!'), or the charismatic, small-time, incidental wise-guys who hassled commuters for travel-cards which they then sold for a fix, or coffee, or jacket potatoes, or a pint and a smoke.

People went in and out of the underground, but Dada's only company were two men, an Ethiopian and a Jamaican, who were both so drunk they could only stay on their feet by hanging on to each other (only two hours earlier, at the Flourmill and Firkin, they'd been total strangers).

'Have you ever studied in your life?' the Ethiopian asked his new friend.

''Cos I have, man,' said the Jamaican, bristling. 'I did paintin'.'

'What is dat?' asked the Ethiopian, tipping backward and forward as if the earth beneath him had turned into the deck of a ship in stormy weather.

'Paintin', just paintin'. Paintin' woodwork, doors, walls.'

Shaking his head, the Ethiopian said: 'Dat's not studyin'.'

'Yes, man, 'cos it is. You can take a course in paintin', ain't it?'

Adamantly, the Ethiopian said: 'Dat's not studyin'.'

'No? You can paint? You can paint? Let me tell you something, can you start a work? Can you rub down a wall, fill it up, paint it and finish it? Can you do dat? Can you fill up every nook and cranny and all dat make de house look like it's brand new?'

'I can,' said the Ethiopian, 'only not perfect.'

'Not perfect!' shouted the Jamaican triumphantly. 'Well, let me tell you something, I can come to your flat and I can say dere needs fillin' up, *dere* needs fillin' up, what a big hole! – You kna I mean – paintin' is no simple ting you know. Anybody could dip a brush in a bloody paint pot and slap it on de wall. Yeah. But you have to go through de preparation. You have to go through de preparation, dat's what I say.'

2

Dada looked at his watch, or rather, at his wrist. His watch had been picked off his wrist in Camberwell Green the week before by a distracted old man who apologized profusely after walking into him.

Dada dug into his pockets and came up with some coins. He shivered to a nearby phone box and dialled.

Nehushta's Call-minder clicked on and her voice, clear as if she were standing beside him, said to him: 'The management regret it has come to their attention that employees dying on the job are failing to fall down. The practice must stop, as it has become impossible to distinguish between death and natural movement of staff. Any employee found dead in an upright position will be dropped from the payroll . . .' A pause, followed by her deep, warm laugh. 'Leave your number, and a message.'

Dada returned to his post and started rolling another smoke.

The two Afro-Diaspora brothers were still at it.

'If you don't help yourself,' the Jamaican was saying, 'nobody is gonna help you. You tink your mother and father is gonna help you?'

It was the Ethiopian's turn to get tetchy. 'Forget about my mother and father.'

His friend did not intend to do so. 'Well, if your mother and father can't help you, who de hell out dere is gonna help you? Who you expect to help you out dere?'

'Who?' the Ethiopian asked – 'De governament' – as if it were self-evident.

'Government?' the Jamaican said, feeling sorry for his friend.

'Yes.'

'What de government doin' right now? They helpin' you?'

'They have to.'

'No, man. Government not helpin' you, man.'

'You have to ask,' suggested the Ethiopian.

'Aks? What you mean aks? You can aks, aks, aks, aks, aks. Aks all you want. You can spend five years of your life aksin' 'nd you still ain't gonna get not'in' from de government. You is a joker, man. Is better you go out dere and try someting yourself.'

'You can petition de governament,' insisted the Ethiopian.

'Petition? You can write a petition to bring it to 10 Downing Street and I guarantee you nine outta ten times it's goin' into de waste-paper basket. You tink say dem look pon we? Youse a joker.'

'What I want is a grant,' stated the Ethiopian, 'to help me to do what I want to do.'

'What is it you want to do?'

'Finish my studyin'. My electronic study. I need to dress.'

The Jamaican eyed him quizzically. 'What are you studyin'?'

'Electronic,' said the Ethiopian.

'You don't need to dress up to do electronics,' his new friend, the Jamaican, who had quite suddenly

sobered up, informed him in deep imponderable
sorrow.

Nehushta appeared freezing, breathless and beam-
ing. 'I'm sorry I'm late. I had to walk. The buses aren't
running.'

Planting a kiss on Dada's lips, which had the
overwhelming and instantaneous effect of sucking all
the anger out of him, she asked, 'Have you been
waiting long?'

'Long,' he said, 'relative to what?' – simply glad to
see her.

Hand in hand, they went down the stairs and into
the underground station.

3

Neither they nor I knew this but it is safe to say that
they fell in love from the very first moment they set
eyes on each other.

They started going out shortly after the choleric
Ras Joseph piss-take appeared in the demotic, multi-
cultural issue of *Cathy*. By now, they had become fast
friends having discovered amongst other things that
they were united in the belief that God made time
sequential just so all trains, from all time, didn't all
arrive in Brixton at the same moment.

They were fascinated by the search for the cure for
Death, wondering whether the deaths that we die every
time we experience an orgasm might not hold the key
to eternal happiness. In which case, should the scientists be contemplating, not the gene of life-everlasting,

but an orgasm-chromosome reticulated into a non-stop clock powered by the sun and set for accuracy on Greenwich Mean Time?

They shared a conceit (which is crucial to the genesis of every relationship, starting from Adam and Eve who in their nakedness thought their weather-beaten skins were Armani suits), that their individual idiosyncrasies, collectively too numerous to mention, would not someday metastasize into the most irritating habits in the whole wide world and on the face of the earth.

They saw movies together and didn't come out hawing in euphemisms.

They laughed out loud on the street and people turned to look. Old ladies smiled at them on the tube.

Which was partly why, after they'd been hanging out for just under a month, he asked her about the state of this relationship she'd told him she was in. She didn't respond immediately (they were out dining at Fukuyama's, her mouth was full, so you see . . .).

'So-so,' she said, reaching for the saké.

'Wanna talk about it?' Dada asked, trying to be a friend but unable to disguise the faint flicker of self-centred, perhaps even self-aggrandizing, hope in his voice.

'No,' she said, picking at her plate.

'Does this person have a name?'

'Rick. Now can we move on to something else?'

So, they moved on to the weather (which, according to Tom Waits in the background, would be 'low clouds with a chance of fog').

He didn't see her, which is to say she avoided him, for a month after that. Then one evening he got back home to find a message on his answering machine. Would he like to go out and do something that weekend?

They caught a Robert Altman double-bill at the Ritzy and moved on from there to the Dog Star on Coldharbour Lane. He had noticed that she wasn't quite as chirpy as usual but knew she'd been working hard of late and put it down to that. Not until she suddenly burst into tears in front of a hundred other people (including a teenage lay-about who became a pop star and remembered the incident forty years later in his Updated Autobiography. He got the bar right, but the city wrong). Not until that happened did it occur to him that all might not be well.

They went to his flat because it was closer than hers.

All she would tell him was that Rick had left for the States and was now history. She wouldn't go into details.

Dada had nipped into Calais via *Le Shuttle* for a few hours the previous weekend and picked up some wine. They went through several bottles of Bordeaux while they talked about a slue of things, including her past (which was peopled with images of her parents and their absence), and his future (which, he said wryly, was being optimistic).

They talked about Luddites and the digital age, of misoneists and miscegenation, of *déjà vu* and tiramisu, and of deserts and the sea, and of Quentin Tarantino films, which they loved and hated. She told him about the bird that saw an aircraft and bowed in worship, he told her about the radio that went into therapy because it was hearing voices. She rolled a smoke. And then another.

He passed out at nine the following morning, just as his neighbour next door commenced on his daily ritual of masturbation. It had long ceased to bother Dada. When he woke up late in the afternoon, she had left.

They met frequently over the next few weeks, twice when he was doing *Cathy* interviews (destined, since he'd soon be sacked, for the pulverizer), and a couple of times at the Lido open-air swimming pool in Brockwell Park. In no time at all, she was back to her crazy old self, the she he knew.

He had invited her along to his tryst with Ras Joseph. When he saw what'd she drawn, he insisted it should go along with his piece in the magazine. She succumbed after he agreed to help her drop off a half of Afghani weed at the stage door of an off West-End theatre for one of her friends who was doing a four-week gig impersonating a Bristol gangster with a Geordie accent, a virtual semiotician, Dolly-the-sheep in dialogue with Charles Darwin, and Tupac Shakur in a Head-to-Head with Pliny the Younger.

Her image accompanied him, like a guard over his solitude, everywhere he went. Her name rolled off his tongue in the lavender-mist of his waking dreams.

The multiculti *Cathy* hit the news-stands on a weekend. Nehushta said never again when she saw her work in print, but he knew she was pleased. To celebrate, they started the evening at SW9, a wine bar and restaurant that took its name from one of the area's postal codes. Later they shifted base to the Dog Star where they ran into the Heckler and a posse of his mates from university. Finally, they ended up at the Fridge, which was holding a pre-millennial retro night of twentieth-century popular music (dating from 1985 which by no coincidence was the year the MC lost his virginity). They danced till the last night bus disappeared into the sharp bend at the top of Effra Road.

Outside the Fridge, as they left the place, Nehushta asked him back to her place for a smoke. He was about to tell her that he was already high as a kite when a voice in his head told him to shut up.

She locked the door when they got to her flat, and began to take his clothes off.

He caught himself that morning listening to his heartbeat but hearing hers. He went into the kitchen and made coffee. The sun was there, too. Darkness had been banished from his heart, and the Cimmerian depths of his soul were awash with light.

4

They walked up the crowded platform on to the escalators, past the ticket barriers, and up a short flight of stairs that spilled them out on to Charing Cross Road, past the Hippodrome and into Leicester Square. A man claiming to be a 'tea leaf', Cockney rhyming slang for thief, was selling a large collection of music

CDs which he said (with a lewd wink at Jann from Cape Town), had come into his possession after they fell off the back of a lorry. 'Darlin' luv,' he said to a French tourist arm-in-arm with her husband, 'what's your favourite position on extramarital sex?'

''Ere, luv, easy-peasy, nice and cushty—' he said to Jann, holding up a Jimi Hendrix, two Bob Marley, one Van Morrison, and a Donna Summer compact disc. 'Five quid for the lot. And a ten per cent discount. I'll make you a walking, talking advertisement for this stand, I will . . . and hurry up, darlin', before the Old Bill comes for *moi*.' He ran through a list of genres represented in his collection: reggae, ragtime, rockabilly, ska, soul and r&b, surf rock, alternative, polka, barbershop, metal, gospel, gothic, indie, jazz, noise, oldies, opera, lounge, blues, choral, cajun, big band, punk, techno, bluegrass, flamenco, folk, funk, new age, new wave, classical, country and western, disco, dixieland, celtic, classic rock, dub, electronica, rap and hip hop, jungle, drum 'n' bass, speed garage . . .

Then, turning to a six-year-old girl lounging happily between her mum and dad, said, 'Oi sweetheart, is your mummy a thief?'

Which at her age, was the most scandalous thing she'd ever heard.

'No, she's not,' she said, sucking her thumb to signal a secret temper tantrum.

'Well, then, m'dear,' said the thief, 'who stole those diamonds and put them in your eyes?'

5

Leicester Square tonight was a neon-lit El Niño of dense but cosy mayhem. They negotiated their way through a parannoying gauntlet of stares from police officers dislodged among civilians by a hoax bomb alert.

A man in a check suit came up to Dada and asked to borrow a pen to take down an address. Dada, not carrying a pen on him, could not assist. The man muttered to himself and went up to a Kiwi tourist.

'Got a pen, mate?'

'No,' said the New Zealander.

'Damn,' said the man in the check suit, shaking his head, 'no one's writing these days.'

'Which one is it?' Dada asked Nehushta.

She reached into her shoulder bag and brought out an invitation card. She looked at it.

'There,' she said, pointing at a multiplex. She sighed and added, 'and we're late,' as if it was his entire fault.

They half-ran into the cinema, flashed their invites at the uniformed ushers and sprinted up a long escalator.

They dashed into the cinema and on to their seats just as the opening credits began to unfold. The title *Burn* appeared in what appeared to be a ball of fire into which the words *written & directed by Ron Althing* dropped like live fish into a frying pan.

'We missed the pre-title sequence,' Nehushta said under her breath.

'It has a pre-title sequence?' Dada, who had not been exactly keen on seeing a movie by his girlfriend's ex-boyfriend, whispered back.

'Yes. About five minutes long.'

'You've seen it before?' He knew she'd seen it before. She'd told him when roping him into attending the preview that, 'I saw a rough edit three months ago. It looked brilliant even then.'

They sat back and watched the rest of the film which, as far as Dada could see, consisted of a succession of fairly well-choreographed car explosions, snappy dialogue coupled with more explosions and snappier dialogue.

6

Sometime later, Nehushta nudged him in the rib. He opened his eyes and was blinded briefly by a shimmering daguerreotype of bleached-out feet shuffling in simian profiles towards the exits, which, in the astigmatic provenance of his sight, took on the shape of a long and narrowing hole that led in a blurred trail across his nose and into infinity and beyond.

Dada woke up with a start and heard the fading ring of the sound of applause. Someone coughed, another person sneezed, and somebody shouted out for Megan to head on for Poons.

7

He sat up suddenly, as the house lights were switched on and the formless daemons on the fringes of his snooze emerged fully bodied in blinks from his eyes, and headed for unknown destinations or the private party in King's Cross.

book four

BOOK four

THE PARTY

1

Their path, from King's Cross station to the arches where the party was being held in nearby St Pancras, was littered with a slurping haemorrhage of human wreckage: worn-out hookers of both sexes, and all the interstices between, shivered in boarded-up doorways, contemplating the hypothesis that youth is wasted on the young, and considered the diseconomies of ageing and the costly algorithm of a good high compared if not contrasted with the price of a cheap wig, which, when worn, made them look cheap *and* glamorous; drugged-up pimps and miscellaneous hustlers negotiated untoward assignations with undercover cops fatally compromised because, well, it's human. Hope seemed available like a room at the Ritz in the glittering phosphorescence of the streetlights and the scrubbed sheen of the kerb-crawling cars.

2

After a five-minute walk in sub-zero conditions and the chill mood of the streets, Nehushta and Dada arrived at a crenellated wall which, when approached, turned out to be a mortised gate that opened on presentation of their invites into a huge, underground space, reached via a spiralling metal stairwell. This cave, packed with guests and booming with the latest mutants of ambient music, led in turn into several other rooms also flooding with guests swinging dis-rhythmically to the riffs devolving from the ubiquitous Tannoy speakers that stared down from the walls. Everyone who mattered and many that didn't in the new-wave elite of the film and entertainment world appeared to be there.

Former geeks, used to staying up nights and into the morning too with naked women conjured up on high-resolution screens in 16-bit High Colour with Matrox Millennium graphics cards and Microsoft DirectX on 21-inch plug and play monitors, congre-gated in corners and talked shop with lapsed nerds recycling tales of being stalked online by virtual squee-gees offering to wash the insides of their degaussed monitor screens for free.

Catwalk-star lookalikes and soap-diva clones smoked herbal cigarettes and walked with panache and sipped glasses of suitably chilled Dom Perignon which, they were told by the movie-mogul aspirants now hitting on them, were made at a place in France called Moet et Chandon.

'The most important part of the process, when the bottles are being aged, is that they must be turned ninety degrees every day. They've got these guys who are professional bottle-turners; they spend three years in apprenticeship, learning the art of turning up to a hundred bottles a minute. As you can guess, this is hard on the wrists so the average span of a bottle-turner's career is seven years. Have you ever wondered why there is that conical indentation in the bottom of champagne bottles?' The women hadn't but it would be uncool, which is to say uncouth, to say so since they knew the question to be a rhetorical one. 'Well, Dom Perignon, the *monsieur* who started it all, realized that carbonation builds up great pressure inside a bottle. When one bottle in the rack bursts, it destroys many bottles around it from the force of the explosion. So he redesigned the bottle, forcing the pressure to escape along the length of the bottle, rather than equally out, so it does not tend to break other bottles in the rack.'

'Wow,' said the women, yawning with their eye-lashes. Their simple and singular aspiration was to be on the catwalks of Paris, London and New York, as well as the cover of *Vogue*, and to drink Dom Perignon with a better class of person, which description did not apply to these guys strutting around oozing reverse charisma, dispensing nuggets of useless erudition, thinking they could blag their way to a quick shag. But useless erudition is anything but useless, especially when it's coming from a man who calls the mythical director Martin Scorseznick 'Marty', and the legendary actor Robert De Jinnius 'Bobby' and claims to have dined out with them only last week at the Soho House. Then, it's called pizzazz, which is an aphrodisiac to which only fools, mystics and the dead are immune (and cave-visiting models too sometimes).

3

Giant screens had been rigged up all over the place and scenes from *Burn* without the audio were projected onto the screens. These as well as a stream of footlights were all the lighting there was.

4

When they finally found Ron, he was talking to a Tokyo film distributor who was telling him in a tactful, circuitous way how much he *didn't* like *Burn*. He did this by talking about the sort of cinema he *did* like:

'Do you know Aki Kaurismäki, of the Finnish movie director?'

'Yes,' said Ron, lighting a cigarette. 'I know his work. Not bad.'

'And Matti Pellonpää of great actor of Finland?'

'Yes,' said Ron. 'I've seen his work. Good man.'

'Let me introduce about them a little,' said the Japanese distributor, who was beginning to get just a mite irritated by Ron's apparent indifference, 'so, they have a lot of fans in Japan, too. Aki spent his youth as a great admirer of movies and, at first, he started his career as an expert of criticism, he made a cinema club and started film-making after a while. His films always move us by their own distinctive way. Matti is great in *Leningrad Cowboys Go America* and *Night on Earth*. His playing characters have their own faults, however, we can't help loving them.

Because he is always expressing eloquently a human merit . . .'

It was at this moment (an opportune one, Ron has asked me to note) that Nehushta appeared with Dada beside her.

'Hush, baby, great to see you!' Ron shouted, throwing his cigarette on the grotto floor and crushing it under his foot.

'It's been nice talking to you,' he said to the Japanese distributor before leaping past him into a long kiss and a tight hug with Nehushta.

'So you're the guy I've heard so much about,' he said grabbing Dada in a warm handshake. 'Lucky devil. I'm Ron.'

'Dada,' said Dada, grinning, disarmed at once.

'As in . . . the Dadaists?'

'No,' said Nehushta.

'All right, I know.' Grinning. 'You did tell me it's a Yoruba name.'

'Where's Simone?' Nehushta inquired.

'She isn't here. Either she's left me or I've left her, we haven't quite decided. But we are both agreed that we've left each other.'

'What happened?' Nehushta sounded, to Dada watching, more like a concerned mother than an ex-lover.

'Oh,' said Ron with a rueful smile, and lighting a cigarette. 'She threw a war and I was the only guest. I guess. Till others came along and the party turned sour. Let's go get some drinks,' he said, leading the way to the bar. 'Did you make it to the screening?'

'Only just,' said Nehushta.

'*And*?'

'I thought it was excellent. Great plot, brilliant set pieces, and great characters except for Mildred—'

'The female lead?' asked Dada.

'Yes,' said Nehushta, 'but I've said this to you before, her character works *despite* your characterization and *because* of what' – spotting across the room, and looking quizzically at her, the actress who played Mildred – '*she* brought to the part.'

'Well, you would say that, wouldn't you?' said Ron in a burst of what sounded to Dada's precontextualized ears like sudden anger, bitterness or a taunt.

If it was a taunt, Nehushta chose to ignore it, and went on to enthuse about everything she liked about the film.

'Wasn't Ricarda' – (who played Mildred) – 'meant to be in the states shooting a movie?' she asked Ron.

'She is,' he replied, 'but she had a few days off so she decided to nip back for this screening. She's flying back first thing tomorrow morning. You wanna go say hello to her?'

'No,' said Nehushta lighting a cigarette.

They were now standing at the bar and sharing a bottle of Ron's favourite poison which, coinciding with Dada's, was red wine. Nehushta excused herself and headed for the ladies'.

'You really hate drinking this stuff don't you?' Ron asked Dada, noticing the speed at which Dada drank his first glass.

'Utterly,' said Dada, refilling his glass.

'Absofuckinglutely. "Hangovers are caused by an absence of alcohol." Jeffrey Bernard.' He picked up an extra bottle of wine. 'Come on, man, let's go rest our butts somewhere. Hush will find us.'

'"Hush?"' Dada repeated, following Ron through the gridlock of bodies.

Ron looked round. 'Didn't she tell you? That's what we all call her.'

Dada assumed that by 'we' he meant Nehushta's friends in the theatre. His nose caught the unmistakable smell of marijuana in the air.

'Is it all right to smoke a joint?'

'Ethically?'

Dada laughed. 'No, I mean, in here.'

Ron brought out a vial from his pocket, poured a pinch of coke into the palm of his hand, which he held against his nostrils sucking the fine white dust into his nose.

'Like some?' he asked, offering Dada the vial.

'No, thanks,' Dada said, reaching for his pouch of weed and, as they found a couple of empty seats, proceeding to roll a cocktail of weed and hand-rolling tobacco.

On the screen nearest to them, a car drove past a billboard that offered the advice: 'Save water, drink Cognac.'

'So, what happens next?' Dada asked, nodding at the screen.

'We've got the UK distribution sorted out, but we're aiming to open in the US first.'

To that end, they were holding a screening the following week for Miramax.

'We're also trying to get it into as many festivals as possible. Best publicity you can buy without having to pay for it. We've got Sundance, Venice, Toronto, and Edinburgh. Tokyo are doing a rain-check, and Cannes haven't got back to us yet. Did you see it tonight?'

Dada had finished building the joint. He borrowed a light from Ron and set it burning.

'I thought it was excellent, a great evening out. One thing that puzzles me though: how come the protagonists survive?'

Ron poured more wine into their glasses, and took a couple of drags from the joint.

'Pretty astute observation,' he said, bringing out the vial once more. 'When we finished cutting the film the first time round, the producers decided on a screening for what they call a trial audience, selected by some sort of social prognostication, who apparently hated the ending because, guess what, everyone dies, so the producers hurled us back in, slammed us against the furniture a few times and told us to go back and re-shoot the ending. I left the meeting seething, and not so much with my tail between my teeth as without a tail at all. That's the bad news, though. The good news is that I think they were right. You know why? Because nobody goes to the cinema to be reminded that someday somehow we're all going to die.' He returned the vial to his pocket, having helped himself to a couple more pinches. 'Hush is right about the

Mildred character, I never did quite get a handle on her. Then again, Mildred was the producers' idea. They wanted a love interest, and it wasn't until the seventh draft of the script that they were able to force me to bring her in.'

At that moment, the actress who played Mildred went past them on her way to the bar. She smiled at Dada and waved at Ron.

Ron waved back and continued, 'Hush is right though. Rick is a fiendishly talented actress. I phoned Hush when we were casting the part and sought her advice. Without a pause, she suggested Rick. I wasn't sold on the idea. I accused her, crudely I have to admit, of trying to make us put our money where her mouth was. She—' Ron stopped, took one look at Dada's face, which had gone a ghostly grey, and went with his eyes shut: 'Shit.' He reached for the vial, poured a heap on his palm and swept it clean with one swipe with his nose. 'I thought you knew,' he said. 'I thought Hush had told you.'

Dada reached for his wine which, because his hand was trembling, Ron had to help him to pick up.

Dada drank up, wiping a trail of non-existent sweat off his face, and stood up.

'It's been a pleasure meeting you, Ron,' he said. 'When Nehushta comes back, tell her that I left.'

Slouched like a troglodyte, he headed for the exit and back on to the mean streets.

5

He knew immediately that he shouldn't have left. He considered going back, turned round to do so, and then remembered that the seven-foot tall gentlemen at the exit had explained to him in plain English, guv, that, for security reasons, anyone who went out would not be let back inside. Which, he tartly responded, meant him as well? If you choose to put it that way, sir, said the superciliously polite Chief Bouncer, making a point of not cracking his knuckles.

He headed back to King's Cross underground station. A roaring confetti of rain tore into his skin like so many soft-ended nails. He was shivering when he reached the station; and slopping in shoes that seemed to have turned into congealed milk laced with barbed wire. He hobbled into a phone booth on the wall of which Pissed Off of Pimlico had etched the counsel: 'Change is inevitable. Except from this coinbox.'

He dialled the Heckler. He wasn't there but his answering machine was on. Dada said, 'Call me,' and hung up. Then he dialled again and added, 'It's urgent,' and rang off.

6

He did not remember getting on the tube, or off it, or walking to his flat, or reaching for the bottle of vodka that had stood on the fridge in his kitchen since Samantha had presented it to him three Christmases ago when they were splitting up (the relationship ended when they started popping up in each other's nightmares). The vodka wasn't so much a parting token of her love as an emblem of her hopes that he would drink himself to death.

The Heckler hadn't phoned and nor had Nehushta.

He dragged the phone to his side and waited for it to ring. He smoked a daisy chain of joints and drank vodka to soothe the dryness of his lungs.

The Heckler didn't phone and nor did Nehushta.

7

Three days later (he thought it was the following morning), still holding on to the phone, his eyes traced a centrifugal swoosh of hand-woven intersecting arcs across the carpet leading like a trail of trenchant wishes to the answering machine across the room, and he saw when he looked that the Full light was blinking. He crawled across the floor and pressed the Play button. He found, to his groggy astonishment, that it was packed full of messages from Nehushta. He'd been in and there all the time and yet hadn't heard the phone ring or the answering machine, which was Designed to Seriously Annoy with the noises it made when intercepting calls. There were in total about ten messages from her, all asking him to call her so she could explain. The Heckler had left a message also, returning his call.

He ran a hot bath, ransacked the flat for anything that was edible, and found among other artefacts a loaf of brown Jamaican bread made *circa* his last but one birthday, tasting when his teeth sank into it like honey-coated plaster of Paris. He got into the bath and fell into a deep sleep-like trance just as he was beginning to feel his strength coming back. When he came to, another day had passed and two miracles had occurred: he hadn't drowned nor caught pneumonia.

He had forgotten to delete the old messages on the answering machine, so there were no new ones. He put on a clean shirt, ran a comb through his hair and stepped out the door to go in search of the Heckler.

8

His body, worn to a frazzle, saw relief in the unseasonably sunny day. It sent signals of warmth to his soul and suddenly it occurred to him as he was standing there, and it hadn't before, that what he should be doing was heading for Nehushta's to apologize for walking off in a huff and abandoning her at the party. She had not, after all, cheated on him. And not telling the whole truth, which was what she had, or hadn't done, wasn't quite the same thing as outright lying or not telling the truth.

Dada stood outside his flat, laughing and crying with relief: I have been a fool, he said to himself, I overreacted. I shall go to Nehushta and say, I've been a fool and a total asshole, please forgive me.

9

It was at this moment, as he decided to stop over at his local florist's to pick up a bunch of roses, daffodils and chrysanthemums and head over to Nehushta's that a man he'd never spoken to before – a man he would shortly know as his neighbour (whom he'd known by the perpetual sounds of do-it-by-yourself coitus emanating from his flat but not by personal acquaintance) came bounding up to him, breathless, his incorrigibly swollen tummy seeming to drag him forward and – thrusting an envelope of black-and-white photographs into Dada's hands – said to him, with ill-concealed glee:

'I'm Haifa Kampana. I thought you might want to see these.'

10

Dada, speechless, glanced at the first photograph, and began to sink again.

THE STALKER

1

Haifa Kampana stalked women he loved.

I do not know when he was born, or where he grew up. Nor do have I much to say concerning his education or the nature of his occupation except to repeat a rumour that explains the source of his income, which has been passed on to me by a friend who runs a café in the Portuguese quarter-mile of Stockwell. One of Haifa's forebears, according to my informant, invented and patented an unspecified household utensil which retails for a pittance but is used in virtually every household in all the cities of the world. Then again, it might have been some other invention. Whatever it was, one of Haifa's parents inherited a half of one per cent of the royalties from this patent, which amounted to a handsome annuity. When his parents died, Haifa being an only child became the sole beneficiary of this endowment.

Haifa moved to Brixton some years ago, after he ran into a woman at the rail station in York where he lived at the time. The woman, who resided in London, was travelling back from Scarborough, where she'd been visiting friends, and was changing trains at York.

Haifa lived within a stone's throw of the station and was stopping by to consult the timetables about a trip to Brighton he was planning to make the following week. He caught sight of the woman as she stepped off the train from Scarborough and was immediately besotted. He bought a newspaper, although his dyslexia prevented him from doing much beside stare at the pictures. He sat down on a bench behind her, and settled down to wait with her for whatever she was waiting for. He followed her, when the London train arrived, and found a seat right behind her. The ticket inspector was sufficiently impressed with Haifa's comportment not to impose a penalty on him for fare evasion. When he asked Haifa where he was going, Haifa smiled, took in the scenery flashing past through the window and said, 'I don't know. I'm following my heart.' The ticket inspector smiled and issued him with a single ticket for all destinations to the train's last stop. The inspector tipped his hat, said, 'Have a pleasant journey, sir,' in a Yorkshire accent and moved on to the next passenger (who as it happened was your storyteller. But that is another tale. If he'd noticed Haifa Kampana, he would have observed a sartorially fastidious man with a sumo-wrestler's protuberance on a midget-child's body. But he didn't. He was listening to the beats of a distant drummer, whose thoughts crashed into his, from a nearby planet visible only to those that dream on high-speed Intercity trains by the grace of Supersaver tickets).

2

At King's Cross the woman went from the mainline concourse down the escalators and on to the Victoria line. She boarded a southbound train. Haifa followed her. He hurried after her when she got off at Brixton, which was just as well; it was the last stop. He saw her struggle with her travel bag and was tempted to approach her and offer to carry it. But caution and cowardice triumphed over this impulsive attack of altruism. She turned left outside the station, though not before buying the *Big Issue* from vendor number 02013 (who used to be a boxer and sparred once, he claimed, with a world-championship contender who fought bravely but was all too often thwarted by the bell). He called the magazine the Biggie and sold it with the following refrain:

> 'Biggie, biggie, biggie!
> Float like a butterfly, sting like a bee-gie
> Your hands can't hit what your eyes can't see-gie
> So, stop right now and buy a Biggie!'

An Italian busker who had spent half an hour outside the tube station mimicking the sound of gunshots and police sirens, which he humbly offered as 'The Brixton National Anthem, ladies and gentlemen,' was now passing a hat round, begging his audience to be generous with their donations. 'This is how I make my living,' he pleaded. 'I don't get money from the government or any other criminal organization.

God bless you.' Haifa glared icily at him and hurried on.

The woman stopped briefly to greet someone in front of Iceland. Her name, Haifa gathered from this phatic exchange, was Susan.

Susan turned into Coldharbour Lane and got into a cab from *Crooks* ('by name, not by nature'), a mini-cab office on the corner of Atlantic Road. A notice on the wall in the cab office, addressed from the 'Customer Relations Department' mused that: 'If we refund your money, replace the goods, sack the manager, close down the store and jump off the nearest bridge, would that satisfy your complaint? Thank you for your custom, please call again.' Haifa was in luck. He jumped into another cab waiting and instructed the driver to follow Susan's cab. 'My wife,' he explained to the cab driver. 'I have reason to believe she has been –' he paused '– foolish.' Susan's destination, it turned out, was only a five-minute ride away. She lived within earshot of a rail station. Trains slid past and you could almost reach out and touch the passengers. Haifa paid off his driver, and with a generous tip. He watched Susan fetch her keys from her purse and walk up to a Victorian house, recently converted into flats. She went inside. He counted imaginary steps until his mind wandered and she disappeared into a void to the back of his thoughts. He did not see her again till the following morning, when she emerged from the house followed by a man about five years younger (she was in her mid-thirties). Haifa, who had stood watch all night, freezing in the fierce winter, had seen the man go in, with his own keys, late the night before. He watched them kiss each other rather perfunctorily on the cheek. The man got into his car and drove off. Susan unlocked a bike leaning against the wall in the hallway and cycled off.

3

Haifa did not attempt to follow her. He walked back to the town centre and asked around until he found a Bed and Breakfast. He got a room, hired a car from a local rental and then went in search of photographic equipment. He stopped by at a bike shop and picked up a sturdy looking two-wheel devil recommended chiefly by its size proportionate to the boot of his car. He went back to the b. & b. and took a nap before hitting the road again, back to his beat on Susan's street.

He spent the night in the car, eyes glued to her door and when she stepped out the following morning he was ready for her with a camera that captured several dozen exposures per minute. Her male friend got into his car and drove off. She got on her bicycle and Haifa followed her on his.

In this way Haifa got to know everything that it was possible to know about Susan without going up to her and asking. He found out where she worked (she was a receptionist at a dentist's surgery), what her pastimes were (she went three times a week to a nearby pub with her boyfriend, played pool or threw darts and was partial to the occasional pint. She had a couple of female friends with whom she went to the movies every weekend. She liked Hollywood blockbusters and thought Mel Gibson was 'gorgeous', and that all his leading ladies were 'slappers').

He found out her most intimate secrets. He followed her once to her GP's and afterwards watched her present the doctor's prescription at a drugstore in return for which she was given a pack of morning-after pills. She bought a litre and a half of Evian Natural Mineral Water.

He started, after this, to masturbate:

He lay on his bed in the Bed and Breakfast and could not go to sleep. He turned this way and that way. He went to the window and looked out onto the street. There was nothing to look at. He turned on the telly and watched, as if he didn't have enough on his mind, an item about how to fit a duvet properly. He shadowboxed until he ran out of breath and was sweating profusely. He brought out the boxes of photographs that he'd developed and printed by himself in a makeshift darkroom he'd set up in his *en suite* bathroom. There were hundreds of them. He laid them on the bed and on the floor and propped others against the wall. His mind, filled with a thousand images of Susan, began slowly and gently to undress her.

4

He reached to her back and unbuckled her bra, slipping it off one shoulder at a time, until she was naked and her nipples, brittle and erect, grazed the tip of his tongue. His manhood rose like a man kneeling standing up. And now, vertically poised, it pushed against his pants, against his trousers and long before his hands, trembling, could reach his zip and pull it down, he experienced a great violence in the lower regions of his stomach and, screaming, he fell poleaxed into the bed and onto the photographs spread out on it like a sea of sand. He lay on his huge rotundity, spent, heaving like a big fish washed ashore.

A moment later, Mrs Henzley his landlady knocked anxiously on his door. She'd heard his scream and images of blood, ambulances and a coroner's verdict of accidental death had crossed her mind.

He stood by the door and without opening it told her that he was all right, he'd merely (mumble, mumble) to his hand. Two days later, she slipped into his room while he was out and came upon the developed negatives of several rolls of film. When he got back the following morning, she looked into the far distance when he greeted her. She avoided his eyes.

5

Three months later, a flat in the house next door to Susan became vacant. Haifa moved in the very next day. He celebrated by treating himself to a slide projector, and a new wardrobe.

As far as he could tell, Susan was completely unaware of his existence. She'd seen him, sure, he'd even held the door open for her once at Marks and Spencer. She'd said, 'Ta,' ever so gracefully and he'd almost ejaculated right there and then. Oh, what a lovely lass. But she'd given no sign of recognition or alarm.

Her boyfriend was another matter altogether. Ever since the morning-after pill episode, which happened again and again, Haifa had developed a bitter, unrelieved hatred for him. Haifa had walked past him on the street a few times and could have sworn the swine had turned round and gazed wonderingly at him.

Haifa set about getting rid of him. To do this, he gave Susan a one-week moratorium, and started to tail Jim the boyfriend instead. He studied his every movement, followed his every step, and, by the end of that week, he knew what to do. He went to a bordello in Streatham one evening and conferred with a hooker for half an hour, which was how long it took him to persuade her to follow him to Jim's watering hole (different from the one he frequented with Susan). But it set Haifa back several hundred pounds and took many weeks and three different hookers before Jim, sloshed one evening, went with this woman who'd told him up-front that she wanted a shag and wasn't it his lucky day. Haifa Photos, Inc. was in the walk-in wardrobe when they got back to the flat he'd rented for the purpose. He sent the prints to Susan by first-class post and two days later Jim and his car were gone, and not too soon and hopefully for ever.

Haifa indulged his *schadenfreude* by treating himself to a pair of heavy-duty binoculars. And a new pair of shoes.

He resumed his old routine. He found that if he

went to an adjacent street and stood at a specific spot, right by a hedge where he could observe unseen, he could see into Susan's back windows, which also happened to be where her bedroom was. He took to going there every night and on a lucky night, thanks to his binoculars, he feasted his eyes on Susan for hours on end.

Haifa was in seventh heaven. He took to eating low-calorie foods and drinking skimmed milk. He bought a belly-cruncher. His stomach rumbled in shock and indignation. Still, he was a happy man. He bought two tickets one for himself, and one for Susan, to see the Chinese National Circus. He saw an invisible asteroid (it was an illusion). He saw a man who weighed eight hundred pounds in money. He saw a giant shorter than a fleeting moment. He sang in the rain on his way back home. When he got home he whistled in front of a mirror. A train slid past. The mirror cracked in two, his smile split in halves. He stopped an officer near Granville Arcade to discuss the drug problem in Brixton and offer some advice. The officer looked him steadily in the eye and then ambled on without so much as a thank you, sir. He saw a documentary on the Battersea Dogs Home and considered adopting a spaniel. The spaniel turned him down.

He'd never been so happy in his life.

6

One evening he turned up at his usual post behind the hedge, set the sights of his binoculars on Susan's bedroom window, and waited for the lights to come on. When he got up, bleary-eyed at dawn the following day, the lights still hadn't come on. He knew what had happened: Susan had not been home that night. He decided that she must have spent the night at one of her friends'.

He only began to worry when a week later there was still no sign of her. He went first thing the following morning to the dental practice where she worked and, on the pretext of booking an appointment for a routine check-up, went inside. He knew, even as he stepped through the door, that she would not be there. And she wasn't. In her place, at the reception, was another woman who, when he asked her, told him she'd taken up Susan's position about a week earlier. She didn't know who Susan was but she'd been told that her predecessor had left suddenly, without tendering her resignation, something to do with a grim depression after the break up of a relationship. Would she be coming back? Haifa asked hopefully. Not as far as I know, said the new receptionist, not unless the practice is expanding and they're planning on having two receptionists.

Haifa went back home and drowned his sorrows in chocolates and ice cream. Three days later, after sending a cheque to his landlord paying several months' rent in advance, he packed a bag and took the next train out to York.

He spent every single day, and several nights too, of the next three months hanging about the main station at York, where he'd first seen her, hoping to catch sight of her.

He spent six months travelling on trains up and down the country and into Scotland and Wales in search of her. He went to Ireland. He flew to Rome, Paris, Ibiza, Tenerife and countless holiday resorts in the Caribbean hoping that he just might run into her somewhere.

He showed her photograph around, telling people she was his sister. Nobody had seen her. In Barcelona, on Las Ramblas – a pedestrian island between two streets – he caught sight of her among the crowds gathered by the flower stalls, jugglers, bird sellers, coin traders, postage-stamp stands and the kiosks selling *Le Monde* and the *Guardian,* the *New Yorker* magazine, the latest Shopping-and-Fucking novels, plus *Playboy* and *Asian Babes*. He gasped after her and into a bar she'd entered and found that she was an English tourist called Sasha. Or perhaps he heard Sabina.

Disconsolate but hopeful still, he decided to go back to London and wait for her. It didn't matter how long it took. He would stay in the same flat, on the same street, and frequent the same pubs and cinemas she had frequented and maybe one day he might run into her.

7

His flat transformed into a numinous shrine to her. He wallpapered the rooms with photographs of her, thousands of them, wall-to-wall. He commissioned a sculptor to build a bust of her, before which he knelt down in supplication once every year on a bank holiday he'd dedicated to her. He set up a giant screen in his living room where the television used to be and watched her every night on the slide projector.

When he sat down to supper every evening, he set the table for two, lit exotic candles and had conversations with her about what she had done during the day. In the background, her favourite musician, Barry Manilow, crooned sunny ballad after sunny ballad.

He commissioned Mr Bill the word-seller of Brixton station, to write a love poem especially for her. Mr Bill meditated for a week then wrote out the line, after carefully parsing it, 'I love you, Susan' fifty times on top-quality heart-shaped photocopying paper and in the finest handwriting. He sent it to Haifa by registered post. Haifa liked it so much he placed it in a national newspaper on Valentine's Day.

He wrote out his will to her.

He masturbated every day to her thousand and one photographs.

He went to the Mezzanine regularly and complained about the prices of things. He did this as a tribute to her: he'd seen her do the same once.

He kept to this routine for three years, unfailingly, and never ever losing hope.

Then he went to the Mezzanine one evening to buy coffee so he could complain about it. And he did.

But that was not all he did. He also set eyes on a new counter-girl called Anna (whose real name was Siobhan).

Back in his flat that night, Haifa exhumed his cameras and dusted them. A week later, he stripped off Susan's pictures from the walls, threw them in a bin liner and flung it in a garbage dump.

Then he developed the forty rolls of film he'd used up during the preceding seven days and, when he printed them, a thousand photographs of Siobhan smiled, frowned, slept and walked past him on every single inch of wall in his flat.

He bought a new evening suit.

8

He observed Siobhan in shots mediated through the lens and shutter-speed of his camera. He followed her the way he used to follow Susan (who by a perverse coincidence suddenly turned up in Brixton three days after he'd gone to Westminster Abbey and pledged his undying love for Siobhan. Haifa reproached God and willed Susan to disappear. Haifa was always reproaching God and, at times like this, God tended to get an earful. God repented and half granted his wish: Susan's soul turned into a pillar of salt. Her body was spotted strolling down the Embankment two weeks later).

Haifa followed Siobhan to her bedsit in Herne Hill. He went with her once on a coach trip to Glasgow when she went back home to spend a weekend with her folks.

On the night most pertinent to our tale of love and loss and the joys of both, it was Siobhan's day off and she spent it indoors in her room with a man who to Haifa's dismay had recently entered her life.

Haifa spent the entire day stationed at the top of Susan's street.

She did eventually come out, round about midnight, with her male friend, who looked, from where Haifa was sitting, to be a little oaf unleashed by an evil spirit disguised as Haifa's karma.

Siobhan and the bastard were dressed up and obviously off to a rave. They headed into town and Haifa followed them. When they got on the tube in Brixton, he got on the next carriage, keeping an eye on them through the separating doors.

They got off at King's Cross. It was pouring heavily with rain when they came out of the station. This didn't seem to bother Siobhan and her friend. As Haifa went past the pool of public phones he saw Dada making his distraught call to the Heckler. Although few of his neighbours actually knew Haifa by sight (he was hardly ever in and when in seldom came out except at night), he knew every thing that it was possible to find out about them. He did this so he could watch out for them during the course of his stalking. And so he recognized Dada when he saw him in the phone booth.

Siobhan and her friend were now crossing the main road. Haifa hurried after them. It turned out they were attending a party in a house on a street off Grays Inn Road. He wandered up and down the street within a short radius of the house, swinging to the occasional wafts of music coming out of the house.

In his mind he and not the pimple-faced squid crawling all over her now was inside at the party with her. And Haifa was thoroughly enjoying himself. When he took to the floor with her, she surprised him with the inventiveness of her dancing, the slick, erotic moves that brought to mind images of go-go dancers from a long forgotten film that Haifa's memory had chosen to record as an actuality from his own past. He decided there and then that he would enrol in a dance class before the year was out.

9

Just before 4 a.m. Siobhan and her friend and several others emerged from the party. Haifa sighed with relief. His teeth were beginning to rattle from the cold. And the party was starting to bore him anyway. He was a non-smoker and a teetotaller; he did not like to be in the company of drinkers and, even less, within breathing distance of smokers.

He got ready to follow them.

But instead of heading towards the main road to catch a night bus, they hurdled into a car, which drove off leaving Haifa feeling not a little betrayed.

He headed back, alone and dejected, toward the station. The underground had long closed for the night but he was sure he would find a black cab. Within

minutes of standing outside the station by the side of
the road, he did manage to flag down a cab.

It was at this moment, as he was taking the few
steps that would bring him into the cab that another
car pulled over and two women, one of whom he
immediately recognized, came out of it. He'd seen
Nehushta with Dada on numerous occasions and knew,
because he'd often heard their cries of passion from his
flat beside Dada's, that they were a couple. He'd also
run into her several times on his surveillance missions
when she was drawing the life forms that gathered like
debris outside the station in Brixton.

He'd never seen the other woman before.

Something about them, plus the fact that he'd seen
Dada earlier that evening looking rather out of kilter,
made Haifa yield to a morbid curiosity. He dismissed
his cab, tipping the driver for the inconvenience. He
walked back to a nearby bus shelter and watched from
there.

The car it seemed had stopped because Nehushta
had insisted on being let out. The other woman was
now trying without much success to persuade her to
get back in the car.

There were two other people in the car, a woman,
driving, and a man sitting beside her. They looked
bemused.

The woman with Nehushta now went round to the
driver's side of the car and said something to her.

'Are you sure?' asked the driver, squeezing her face
and glancing at the man beside her as if to say, 'Do
you think we should leave them here?' To which the

man's face seemed to respond: 'Yes, I think they want to be left alone.' All the same he leaned out and shouted, 'For God's sakes, Hush, this is King's Cross and it's four in the morning!'

'Go on,' said the other woman, 'we'll be fine.'

'You sure, Rick?' asked the driver, looking quite concerned.

'Yes,' said Rick, bending over to give her two quick pecks on the cheeks. 'We'll be all right, trust me. My flight's at ten. I'll either phone or send you an e-mail from New York.'

'I know you're sick of hearing this, but you were brilliant in the film,' said the man.

She laughed, they kissed and the car drove off.

She went back to Nehushta.

'Listen, Hush,' she said. 'We'll grab a cab to my place and talk, okay?'

Nehushta said nothing.

'All right, honey?'

Nehushta, looking tearful and angry, did not respond.

A black cab pulled into a rank nearby and Rick ran up to it, pulling Nehushta tentatively by the arm. Haifa's luck with public transport did not desert him that night. Another cab arrived and he jumped into it. 'Follow them,' he ordered the driver in an authoritative voice and quickly flashing his season travelcard as if it were a detective's id. 'Covert duties,' he added just in case the man was in a foul mood.

10

They drove down Euston Road on to Marylebone High Street, turning into Edgware Road and off into a meandering succession of contiguous side streets that brought them finally into a quiet, tree-lined avenue in West London. Rick, followed by Nehushta, got out. Rick paid the driver and they went through a little wooden gate leading to a white, Elizabethan house overgrown with foliage.

As Haifa scrambled out of his cab, tucking a ten-pound note into the driver's hand, he saw the two women standing by the door of the house, Rick reaching into her shoulder bag presumably for her keys. Nehushta turned side-ways and looked out on to the street. Haifa walked straight on and doubled back a moment later. He slipped through the gate of the house next door, separated from Rick's by a short wall and tall, bushy climbing plants. He listened for the presence of dogs and, satisfied there were none, moved close to the wall and peeped through the plants.

He thought at first that one of them had gone inside and that the other, for whatever reason had chosen to remain outside. Then he realized they were both still there outside the door. The reason he'd thought that he was seeing just one person was because they were now engaged in a passionate French kiss. He held his breath and watched.

A few minutes later, he negotiated his way back on to the street, into Rick's house and through to the back of the house which revealed itself to be a cornucopia of sprawling plants. The house was split into six flats, and Rick's, to his right, was on the ground floor. As the lights, first in the hallway, then in the kitchen, and then the living room followed by the bedroom came on one after the other, Haifa almost jumped for joy: he could see clearly into practically every room in the house except perhaps the bathroom. The curtains were either half-drawn or not drawn at all.

Haifa watched them. They were now in the kitchen exchanging a heated barrage of words. Nehushta lashed out at Rick and struck her across the face. It appeared that the kisses outside had been merely a temporary outbreak of peace and not wholesale rapprochement. A Bloody Mary, which Rick had been making, dropped from her hands and crashed on the floor. Nehushta stormed out of the kitchen crying and wailing and into the living room, followed a moment later by Rick screaming and swearing at her. Tears, followed by more recrimination, culminated again in a suffocating embrace, suffused in equal measure with love and indignation, and a kiss that morphed into a beige-tinted chiaroscuro stereopticon of urgent, combustible sex which, long after it was over, and the two women had fallen asleep in each other's arms, left Haifa shivering not from the cold but from shock and in hyperventilation.

11

Haifa auto-focussed and began to snap.

THE PLAGUE

1

Dada stood outside his flat rifling slowly through the photographs Haifa Kampana had handed to him. He had been standing there, with Haifa breathing heavily beside him, for less than a minute. His tongue had gone dry and when he asked, in a voice he could hardly recognize as his own, how Haifa had come by the photographs his ears did not register a single word of Haifa's hastily mumbled explanation. Haifa told him that he was a freelance newspaper photographer and that he had stumbled on the sight of Nehushta and her lover while covering an assignment involving a philandering celebrity in a house nearby. He had decided to hand over the photographs, he said, because he personally had no use for them. He had considered destroying them (which, in truth, he had), but had decided that to be true to his conscience and in the spirit of good neighbourliness, to knock on Dada's door and hand them over, prints, negatives and all.

The truth was that Haifa had woken up that morning feeling very depressed for the second day in a row. He had discovered only the day before, having followed his beloved Siobhan to an appointment with her General Practitioner, that she was pregnant. He had watched her and her abominable boyfriend as they celebrated the news. Haifa's fury knew no bounds. And his humiliation, because he felt cuckolded, was so deep he went back home after the tragic news and covered his face in shame. He used a pillow to do so. His heart had lightened slightly only when, a few hours earlier, he remembered the photographs he'd taken in west London on the night of the party. His heart lightened and his feet danced into his darkroom when he considered the prospect of passing a little of his misery round. After all, he decided, he didn't hold the monopoly on misery. He would develop the negatives, make some prints and put them in an envelope and shove them through Dada's post box, then he would hang around incognito and when Dada had seen them and hopefully set out for Nehushta's with murder on his mind (or Grievous Bodily Harm, at the least), he would have the pleasure of knowing that right next door to him lived a man even more miserable than himself. But all had not gone completely according to plan. When he ran out of his flat and headed for the flat next door he'd been so excited about his nifty little plan that he hadn't bothered to look up and by the time he did he was staring right into his neighbour's face. Haifa prided himself in being an accomplished and convincing liar, but he needed time to prepare his truths and to rehearse his spontaneity. He was practically useless when caught out on a limb, which was what happened to him when he looked up that morning and found himself in front of Dada's door and breathing into Dada's face. His hands shot out of their own volition and thrust the photographs into Dada's hands and his voice, independent of his mind, announced: 'I'm Haifa Kampana. I thought you might want to see these.'

He counted the next several seconds in geological time and to the spluttering of his frightened heart. Supposing, he thought, the man physically unleashed his fury on him? Even worse, supposing he decided to call the police?

He stood there trembling ever so slightly, waiting for Dada to speak.

Dada reached into his trouser pocket, ensnared a crumpled, half-smoked spliff between his thumb and little finger and inserted it between his lips. He lit the spliff, smoked thoughtfully for a while, and then he handed the photographs back to Haifa.

'Keep them or destroy them, do what you will with them, Mr Kampana. They're of no use to me.'

He finished smoking the spliff, crushed the roach under his foot, and headed into Brixton in search of the Heckler.

2

The evangelists today were a duo of young black men dressed in long flowing gowns who belonged, their board attested, to the Twelve Tribes of Israel. Their accent was African-American by way of Derby.

'God ain't gatherin' no Christian group,' declared the Preacher. 'He ain't gatherin' no Church. First of all

Church is a Greek word "Glatia" that means gatherin'
of people. We're the people that the Most High's
gatherin'.' He turned to his assistant. 'Read.'

The assistant lifted his well-thumbed Bible and
began reading:

' "Gather my saints together unto me. Those that
have made a covenant with me by sacrifice." '

' "And made a covenant with me by sacrifice," ' the
Preacher noted. 'Moses and the Israelites. Those are the
saints of the Most High. Give me Psalms 1, 48 and 14
. . . The only saints of this Bible is you so-called
Negroes. You West Indians, the Haitians, Dominicans,
the Puerto Ricans, the North American Indians. Those
are the saints of the Bible. Those are the Israelites.
Those are the Jews. OK? A lot of you so-called black
men you go, "Oh, I ain't no Jew." You *are* the Jews
that the Bible speaks of, OK. Archaeology and histori-
cal records testify to this. Not just me and my big
mouth. I'm coming out of the Bible with facts. Read.'

'Psalms 1, 48 and 14, "He also exalted his people." '

'That's who the Most High's gonna exalt in these
last days. The Israelites, his people. You so-called
Negroes. We're gonna be exalted as a people on the
Planet Earth. And all the Nations gonna know that
we're the Israelites. All the Nations gonna know that
we're the Lord's chosen people in these last days.
Read.'

' "The praise of all His Saints. Even the Children of
Israel." '

'That's who are the Lord's saints?'

'The children of Israel.'

'Did he say the white man?'

'The children of Israel.'

'Did he say the Chinese Japanese?'

'The children of Israel.'

'Did he say the Arabs?'

'The children of Israel.'

'That's who the Lord's saints are – the children of Israel. Who *are* you so-called Negroes, you West Indians, Dominicans, Puerto Ricans – that's who the saints are. The children of Israel. OK? Give me Romans the third chapter and the first verse. The whole world is for the Israelites. And the Israelites is coming back on the Earth to set up righteousness and to set up the Law, statutes and commandments that's found in the Bible. That's who we're gonna give. OK? Right now we're in the talkin' stage. We're in the preachin' stage. We're in the gatherin' stage. But soon it's gonna be the killin' stage. OK? Christ is comin' with the Heavenly Host – mighty warriors! OK? The Top Gladiators of the Universe. The Angels. And he's comin' to set up laws, statutes and commandments on this Planet Earth like you ain't never seen. The Lord said he's gonna work a work in your days that you ain't gonna believe. Look at all the floods that's goin' down in America. Look at all the bombs and terrorism that's goin' on on the earth that you walk on, in your daily life, like everythin's OK. Why, because it didn't hit your front door yet. But when it does hit your doorstep don't be shocked. Don't be terrified, 'cos you was warned. OK? You was warned and you was told these things. That's when you're gonna know there's been a prophet among you. Because you're gonna be already told. Read.'

'Romans 3 and 1, "What advantage then have the Jew?"'

'What advantage is there to bein' a Jew or an Israelite? You so-called Negroes, 'cos you don't believe that you're a Jew. You so-called black people, you don't believe that you're the Israelites—'

'I know I'm a Jew,' declared a black woman in the gathering.

'That's good,' said the Preacher. 'That's good – all right.'

'I praise the Lord!' said the black Jew.

'Yeah, now if you believe that, you gotta come and learn. OK—'

'Well, give me your card and I come to your church,' said the woman.

'It's right here, OK. Now you have to come and learn sister, that's beautiful. The Lord—'

'Thank you,' said the woman, swaying slightly on her feet. She was drunk.

'The Lord is gatherin' his people together and he wants us to come back and do what's right. Not to gather yourself to no religion. OK. The Lord ain't gatherin' – he never set up no religion. Read.'

'"What advantage have the Jew? Or the profit of circumcision?"'

'What is the profit of being circumcised? When the circumcision, of keepin' the laws, statutes and commandments that the Heavenly Father set. What profit is this – read.'

'Much every way,' said the assistant.

'What?'

'Much *every* way.'

'Much every way. Because the Israelites the Jews, when we get the earth, when the so-called black Americans and Negroes, the West Indians, the Haitians, the Dominicans, Puerto Ricans, the North American Indians, the Cubans, Ecuadorians, all the way down to the Mexicans, when we get the earth back again, we gon' control everythin'. OK. The Kingdom of Heaven is only for one people. Only for one people – and that's it. We been taught the Kingdom of Heaven's for everybody – but it don't say that in the Bible. Read.'

'I believe what he said!' shouted the black woman. 'I believe! My mammy taught me this way – my mammy's a Christian. She taught me that.'

'Much every way,' agreed the assistant. 'Chiefly because "unto them were committed the oracles of God."'

'Because unto them was given the oracles of the Most High. The oracles of God are the laws, statutes and commandments. And that was only given to one people. OK. First of all, Christ didn't come for all these nations, he came for one people. He was only the saviour of one nation. According to the Bible. We gon' read that for you—'

'Can I ask you a question, please?' asked the woman.

'Er—'

'Do you know most of these people who sayin' they

is pastor and preach in the church, they're the more Devil?'

'Yeah,' agreed the Preacher.

'You know dat!' The woman looked ecstatic – it was as if no one had ever agreed with her before.

'Yes. OK,' said the Preacher.

'I went to church last Sunday. And if I'm sick, they're supposed to 'eal me and dem wan' trow me out.'

'That's right. The Bible says—'

'Dem are no God,' declared the woman, still smarting from the incident.

'The Bible says if you sick you're supposed to take the oil and anoint your head and pray. OK. The elders in the church are supposed to come and pray with you. You been taught that you're nobody. You're on the bottom. That's why Christ said, the last is gon' be first. And those that first, gon' be last. Read.'

' "When John had first preached, before his coming, the baptism of repentance, to all the people of Israel." '

'Repentance for all the people of Israel. That's who repentance is for OK? For you so-called Negroes, you West Indians. Why? Because you went against your Father. OK. You went against your Heavenly Father. You didn't keep his laws, statutes and commandments. You didn't teach your children *diligently* what they are supposed to do, what they were supposed to eat, how they were supposed to act. That's why your children run around mad. That's why they go around acting up. Why – 'cos they haven't been *taught*. What haven't they been taught? They haven't been taught the rules

and regulations, outta the Bible. If your child acts up
the Bible says you supposed to beat them. Beat them
and show them the right way and train up your child
and the way he shall go and when he is old he will not
depart from you. OK? Read.'

'Don't spare de rod an' spoil de chile!'

'"For when John had first preached before his
coming, of the baptism of repentance to all the people
of Israel, and John fulfilled his cause, he said: whom
you think I am, I am not he, but behold, there cometh
one after me, whose shoes on his feet I am not worthy
to loose."

'Just like John was preparin' the way, we preparin'
the way. OK? And we supposed to come out here and
tell you so-called Negroes that you are the Israelites
that the Bible is speakin' of. You ain't supposed to be
goin' into no other philosophy or religion. OK? The
Bible never taught that. Get that straight. OK? All
these religions, philosophies, Islam, Holy Tabernacle,
Baptist, Methodist, Rastafarian, they're *all* false. All of
them false and man-made. One of the main things that
our people go into, they go into Islam. OK? The
Nation of Islam, they wanna be a Arab. That's a Arab
philosophy. How you gon go into a Arab philosophy
when it was the Arabs, the Africans and the Arabs—'

'That's absolute rubbish!' shouted a black Muslim
man.

' – that was sellin' your behind on the West Coast
of Africa. This is the facts OK. This ain't rubbish, this
is the facts! Arabs that was sellin' you so-called black
men into captivity into slavery.'

'He showin' you de way!' the woman reproached the Muslim man.

'Racist!' screamed the Muslim.

'Shut up!' the woman hollered at him.

3

Dada wandered off from the Twelve Tribes excoriation, as the slanging match between the Muslim and the Preacher, backed by the woman, began to lurch from jousting tragicomedy into a minor public disturbance. One thing was certain: the Heckler was not there. He was nowhere to be found.

'You're sweating like a shower door!'

He swung round to find Midé examining him with exaggerated but real concern.

'Where've you been man? I've been phoning you for three days solid, couldn't get through, couldn't leave a message 'cos that answering thing of yours is full.'

'I've been lying low,' Dada said. 'Seen my cousin anywhere?'

'That's why I've been phoning you. He's at my place, and he's been asking for you.'

'Why's he at your place?' Dada asked, his heart sinking because he knew the answer.

'Three days ago,' said Midé, 'while having it out with one of those cranks by the station he fell into what looked like an epileptic fit. By pure chance, I was walking past when it happened. Since I knew he'd tested positive two years ago and hadn't fallen ill since the test, I knew this was probably the first big *pow* by the Fearsome 'A' on his immune system. The doctors confirmed it at the hospital. They put him on drips and a whole encyclopædia of drugs. He pulled out of it within a day and by noon yesterday he was fit to go home. He wanted to come to your place but since you seemed to have faded from the face of the earth, I told him he could come to mine and stay until you reappeared as long as he promised to listen to my jokes and not tell me they stank.'

They arrived at Midé's flat. It was in a basement right next door to his bookshop. The flat was decorated with artwork and relics he'd picked up while on holidays in Trinidad where his parents were from. They went through the kitchen to reach the living room. Hanging on the kitchen wall a photograph of the writer Sam Selvon, in profile, smoke rising from a cigarette in his hand, reading from his fifties master-piece *The Lonely Londoners*.

The Heckler was stretched out on the couch in the living room, head resting on a pillow placed on the armrest. He was watching a video on Midé's giant television set, which Midé had bought solely to watch cricket test matches, football and the Comedy Channel, in constantly alternating order.

Dada sighed and paused by the door when he saw on the screen what his cousin was watching. He was watching the video of a birthday party for Andre, his lover whose death soon after the party had prompted the Heckler to make the trek to Jefferiss Wing, the Sexually Transmitted Diseases arm of St

Mary's hospital in Paddington. Within weeks of being told he was HIV positive, he quit his high-flying job with a software company, was kicked out of his flat (for not paying his rent. That's when he moved back in with his mother, and became the Heckler. That also was when Dada's intimate love affair began with the bottle).

Andre, in drag, was doing his *Marilyn Monroe Unplugged!* act. Dada caught a brief glimpse of Samantha and himself in the background, applauding with the other guests as the Heckler, as Billie Holiday, joined Andre in a duet on a Fats Waller song called *You're Not the Only Oyster in the Stew*:

> You're not the only oyster in the stew;
> you're not the only apple on the tree.
> However, I'm convinced,
> completely, fully, firmly convinced:
> You're the only one for me . . .

The Heckler felt their presence and looked around from the couch. Apart from a certain fragility manifested in the rubicund tiredness of his eyes, the illness had yet to proclaim itself physically on his features.

'Let me take a guess,' said the Heckler after one look at Dada's dishevelled appearance. 'She dumped you, didn't she?' He sprang up, landed rather gingerly on his feet and came to Dada, his thin frame slightly hunched over. He grabbed Dada by the wrist and pulled him to the couch. 'Sit down here and tell your Agony Aunt all about it.'

Dada smiled weakly. 'Midé told me about what happened,' he said. 'I'm sorry you couldn't reach me.'

'Listen, punk,' the Heckler reached for the remote control and turned the volume down. 'I'm utterly and completely fine now. In fact, I feel so fine I'm gonna punch you if you don't start talking. Man, you look terrible!' Turning to Midé, 'Doesn't he look terrible? I think he deserves a drink for looking so terrible.'

Midé fetched a bottle of Trinidadian rum from the kitchen.

He poured three glasses.

Dada talked without interruption save for the Heckler's constant, 'Well, well, well.'

When he finished, Midé said, in a faux cockney accent, 'You wos had, matey.'

'Two things,' said the Heckler. 'First, you shouldn't have left the party. That was dumb, and, if I may say so, and I think I can, childish. Two' – he grabbed the phone – 'call Nehushta. Hear what she has to say. Who knows, you might be lucky: have you ever considered being the well-endowed member – pardon the puns – of a divine *ménage à trois*?'

'I'm not going to phone her,' Dada said.

'Why not?'

'Because I don't feel like it.'

'That's a good reason, my dear Knight-of-the-square-table. But you've still got to deal with the situation. And the best way to do this is by talking to her. If it's over between the two of you, then shed the tears, look your life in the face, pick the pieces off the floor, say to the past "thanks for calling," put on

275

the best frock you can buy, borrow or steal then step out the door and into the future. End of story. But first' – placing the phone on Dada's lap – 'phone the bitch.'

Dada took a deep breath and dialled.

The Heckler lit a cigarette.

'Don't stay too long on the phone,' he advised, flicking ash into an empty glass. 'And don't burst into tears either, she might think you've lost it and refuse to meet you. Arrange to meet somewhere neutral, then when you see her, put your thumb in your mouth and start rolling on the floor.'

Midé laughed.

Dada had the phone glued to his ear for a while then he put it down slowly.

'Why didn't you leave a message?' the Heckler asked.

'She's gone off to the States,' he said listlessly. 'She left a New York number.'

Even the Heckler looked disappointed.

'She's got no style,' he said, trying to console Dada. Then, 'Did she say when she'll be back?'

'No.'

The Heckler turned to Midé:

'Got any smoke?'

'You know I don't smoke that stuff.'

'Oh yes, I forgot,' looking downcast, he turned to Dada. 'I'm really going to miss her.'

Dada was moved close to tears by his cousin's simpatico.

'She sold such sweet marijuana,' the Heckler said,

taking a last drag at his cigarette. He squashed the stub in the improvised ashtray. 'My regular dealer,' he said, 'got nicked last week.'

'*C'est la vie*,' he sighed bitterly. 'I'm sorry, guys. I'm just feeling Sad about Sarajevo.' This was his term for simple, debilitating, low-level every day blues. Then, looking at the screen: 'I miss Andre. I miss him so much.'

The images on the screen had changed from those of a birthday to scenes from a funeral. Andre's photograph, draped with flowers, placed above his coffin lying on the altar of a chapel in North London. Dada remembered being there, and also operating the camcorder. The Heckler had requested Louis 'Satchmo' Armstrong's *St James Infirmary* as the last piece of music to be played. Satchmo's gravelly, undeniably uplifting voice, now roared at them quietly from Midé's Dolby-Surround system:

> 'I went down to St James Infirmary
> Saw my baby there.
> She was stretched out on a long, white table:
> So cold, so sweet, so fair.
>
> Let her go, let her go (God bless her!),
> Wherever she may be
> She can look this wide world over:
> but she'll never find a sweet man like me
>   (just bragging!) . . .'

4

The Heckler was weeping. Dada held him to his chest, rubbing his neck, letting him cry.

book five

THE FLIGHT

1

On the day Nehushta phoned, Dada was a roiled wreck of motile anticipation when he woke up. The traffic lights at the crossroads between the High Street and Stockwell Road blew a fuse. He'd had a strange and incomprehensible dream during the night. He'd heard voices in his sleep. They were coming from his head.

2

In the morning, he heard Haifa Kampana beseeching a hank of onions to please stop trespassing on his mind.

3

He had lunch with the Heckler. All things considered, the Heckler seemed well.

4

That evening Dada met up with Nehushta at the Brixtonioso restaurant. The Brixtonioso was situated above the Ritzy cinema, and although it had its own

entrance, Dada often preferred to approach it via the
Ritzy's foyer. He has asked me to point out (apropos
of nothing, I should say) that Isaac Hayes' *'The Theme
from "Shaft"'* was playing on the public address system
when he stepped through the front-of-house box office
area into the foyer. As he turned right and pushed the
doors opening to the stairs that led up to the restaurant, Mr Hayes stopped him in mid-track with the
question:

> 'Who's the black private dick
> That's a sex machine
> To all the chicks?'

'Shaft,' Dada responded.

'You're damn right,' said Isaac Hayes.

She was five minutes late. Five minutes and six
months to be precise, he said when she started apolo-
gizing. A look of near exasperation flashed briefly across
her eyes. Then she smiled, sat down and peeked at the
wine list. He told her she looked beautiful. She replied,
'I know,' then smiled and thanked him. You're not
looking too bad yourself, she said returning the com-
pliment and *ipso facto* telling the first and only lie of
the evening. She had acquired a hint of Gotham in the
cadence of her speech.

5

As the ice thawed between them, and the initial
tentativeness gave way to honest spontaneity, and

serious frivolity, and the wine arrived, and she brought out a cigarette and he leaned across and lit it for her, and they flirted good-naturedly with each other, rambling about this and then about that, without actually talking about the thing that had brought them here, several things struck me as I, Mr Bill, the word-seller of Brixton, observed them in my thoughts and walked away to tend to other matters implicated in the blistering heat of my existence. I realized that they too realized that by the end of the evening, having dissected and deconstructed, analysed and re-examined the facts of the matter, they would agree to disagree. He would go his way, and she would go her way. But they would factor a friendship of sorts. In a few years he would receive an invite in the post, to her *Brixton* exhibition at the 198 gallery. She would introduce him to Rick. They would natter like old friends. He would ask her if she still sold weed, and she would laugh and say no, not since it became freely available on doctor's prescription. He would ask if she'd lately seen Ron. He'd gone on to write more plays and more films and become wealthy enough to stay the occasional weekend at the Betty Ford clinic.

She would ask after the Heckler. He would tell her about his cousin: how he was no longer the Heckler, having come to terms with his demons, entered a new relationship, got his act together and gone back to his old job. Aunt Moni, delighted, was convinced it was her prayers and the faux funeral that had made it all happen. The Heckler (now 'Biodun) hadn't still told her about his illness. He would tell her, he said, when the time was right. He'd been saying that for years. He too would have been at Nehushta's private viewing that evening, but for a date he had with his boyfriend. Midé never quite hacked it as a stand-up, but his bookshop continued to thrive.

Dada never did write the book of verse. But in time he would write a book about Brixton, about the weird and wonderful, sometimes saddening, constantly exhilarating characters that people the streets of Brixton and give it that strange, phantasmagoric quality which is called surreal. He would have at the book's heart several people reaching out to one another, searching for love. Sometimes being thwarted and sometimes not.

He would examine, on Mr Bill Gates' Windows graphical user interface, the character of His Royal Creepiness Haifa Kampana, whose fictive names he would pick at random from a list of computer viruses – a stalker being by definition analogous to a computer virus, which, I am told, is a programme that attaches itself, uninvited, to another programme. With the aid of the word processor, Dada would cut Haifa here, paste him there; he would adumbrate him at the beginning of the story, and introduce him properly only toward the end. Haifa Kampana – be it noted – ended his stalking career six months into Siobhan's pregnancy. He awoke one morning, and armed with several litres of gasoline and a cigarette lighter, which he had bought specially for the purpose, went and stood outside the Mezzanine and, in protest at his betrayal by Siobhan, doused himself in the liquid and set himself on fire. He suffered severe burns but was rescued before it was too late. A tabloid newspaper reporting the incident ran the story under the morbidly gleeful headline, 'Brixton Bar-B-Q!' Haifa Kampana ended his days in a psychiatric hospital from where he took out a life-long subscription to *Cathy* magazine.

6

As I write these words down with a black biro on a lined notebook at my tiny desk in my home down under Waterloo Bridge, a dog barks in the distance. A freight lorry rumbles past. It's a clear sky tonight, and if I look deep into my heart, I may spot the Pleiades, that dazzling cluster of small stars in the constellation Taurus, seven of which are discernible by the naked eye.

7

Earlier that day, Dada had been so sure Nehushta would phone he endowed every tiny incident, from the whistling of a boiling kettle to the thin high-pitched calls of a distant flock of siskins, with the magnitude of prophecy. But he kept this to himself.

When the phone finally rang, he was on the sofa in his flat, unwinding with a smoke and re-running in his mind a screening of the 1970s Jamaican cult classic *The Harder They Come* starring the reggae singer Jimmy Cliff. You believe him can help you more than me? asked the local police chief, bristling with rage. No, said the poor stoolie who had incurred the chief's displeasure. Then what the backside you go and do that for? barked the policeman. Jimmy Cliff was carefree and cool and irredeemably very sixties.

8

The phone rang and Dada snapped out of his evening-out-at-the-movies.

'Who dat?' he asked, knowing even before she said a word who it was.

'Hi, Dada,' she sounded as if she were next door.

He sat up, feeling a trifle woozy.

'Hello, stranger,' he said into the mouthpiece.

'What are you doing?' she asked, a tentative smile and a real awkwardness layering her voice.

'Watching a film,' he said without thinking.

'You bought a new telly?'

'Yes . . . I mean no,' he said, 'just playing one of my total-recall games.'

'This is weird,' he continued hurriedly as he realized he might have given her reason now to think that he had so much time on his hands he'd taken to vegetating on his sofa, and – worse even – in front of a non-existent television set. 'This is strange, and you may not believe it, but I knew when I woke up this morning that you would phone sometime today.'

She sounded slightly puzzled: 'I phoned you last night and said I'd call again this evening.'

You did? he screamed silently.

'Don't you remember? I called last night; you sounded sleepy so I said I'd call today. I flew in from the States three days ago.'

He had no recollection whatsoever of having talked to her but at least it accounted for the voices he'd heard in his head.

'I must have been in deep sleep,' he said. 'I don't remember speaking to you.'

9

The truth, which he knew she might have guessed, was that he'd been resolutely *non compos mentis*, which is to say plastered, the night before. On top of which he had sampled numerous skunks originating from the Swiss mountains, brought to his attention by his versatile new dealer, an eighteen-year-old Bosnian Serb whose sole purchase on the English language consisted of the words, 'I quit understand,' which he cheerfully uttered in all circumstances bar none. His papers presented him as Goran, but he answered to the sobriquet Quit.

10

Dada was glad, though, to be disabused of the illusion that he might be developing psychic powers. When the phone rang just now and it was Nehushta on the line, he had thought for a moment that Aunt Moni and her God, just to see the look on his face, might have cooked up this prophecy fulfilment. Aunt Moni had recently taken to pestering him with calls urging him to find time to speak to God.

'People get sectioned, Auntie, they get locked up in mental hospitals, when they start speaking to God,' he told her.

She was used by now to his cheap sarcasm. She informed him calmly that we spoke to God through prayer, by opening our minds to Him.

'I'd feel pretty stupid, Auntie, shutting my eyes while speaking to something that I couldn't see anyway, even if my eyes were open.'

'God is not 'something,'' she rebuked him. 'He is omnipresent and omniscient, the Alpha and the Omega.'

'If he's such a Houdini, Auntie, what he needs isn't a word with me, but a prime-time slot on ITV.'

'That's negative communication with the Almighty, Dada, it's worse than not praying at all.'

Aunt Moni had recently enrolled on a foundation course with the Open University and since then she'd started coming out with strange terms.

'What is negative communication, Auntie?'

'That's how Salman Rushdie started. See where it got him,' she said ominously. 'I will pray for you.' And slammed down the phone.

11

'Are you there?' Nehushta asked.

'Yes . . . sorry.' It was all coming back to him. 'Of course . . .' We said we might meet up at the Brixtonioso this evening, right?'

'Yes,' she said. 'And I said I'd phone to confirm.'

'And?'

'What?'

'Are we still on?'

'You mean . . . for this evening?'

'Yes.'

'I am, if you are.'

'Okay. See you later.'

'Dada?'

'Yes?'

'We didn't say what time.'

'Oh. How about – ' He checked his wrist and discovered for the millionth time that he had no watch.

'Nine?' she suggested.

'Nine is great,' he said. 'What time have you got?'

She told him it was five past eight.

'See you in just under an hour.'

Immediately she rang off he phoned the Heckler.

'She phoned,' he said. 'I just spoke to her.'

'Try speaking one word then the next,' the Heckler advised him. 'Who phoned?'

'Nehushta.'

'Ah.'

'That's what I thought, "ah". I'm meeting her later this evening. What do you think?'

'Well, my dear coz, as my dear mum, your dear aunt, would say, "Go with God."'

'Seriously, 'Biodun: what do you think?'

'I want a blow-by-blow account of the meeting on my desk first thing tomorrow morning.'

'Will do, sir.'

He put the phone down and went into the bathroom. Haifa Kampana yawned next door (the walls were so thin not only could Dada hear him think, he could hear him change his mind).

12

As Dada stepped out the front door and on to the street, and headed for the Brixtonioso, an alien thought began to take shape in his mind. It assumed the form of an invisible weight pulling him down and crushing him at the same time. He decided, on a whim, to flee from his mind. He soared into the night, like a scream rising, and up to the stars.

13

Then he changed his mind – into a pair of eyes. They stared dimly at him, as he walked along the street.